THE MAGICAL

BY the BOOK

LIZ HEDGECOCK

WHITE
RHINO
BOOKS

For Ruth,
my first and fastest beta reader

Chapter 1

'What do you think?'

Jemma stepped back and surveyed the window display of The Friendly Bookshop. The mantelpiece, carefully constructed from cream-painted cardboard, held four woollen stockings, and out of each peeped a book. A Christmas tree stood to the side, under which were various book-shaped parcels; every day, a parcel would be opened to display the book within. The background of the display was hung with garlands and candy canes.

She looked outside, where Maddy and Luke were whispering together. *Off in a world of their own again.* She rapped on the window, then pointed at the fireplace.

They disengaged themselves long enough to give her a thumbs up, then wandered in. Jemma walked outside to see the effect. *Yes, that will do nicely.*

'It's lovely,' Maddy ventured when she came back

inside. 'It's so nice to have a Christmas display.' A pause. 'Brian never saw the point. He said that the books would sell themselves anyway, whatever the season.' She managed a trembling smile which died quickly, like a guttering candle.

'He's right in some ways,' said Jemma. 'It isn't as if we don't sell books the rest of the year. Speaking of selling books, I need you to come to Burns Books with me, Luke. Raphael's going on a book-buying trip, remember?'

Luke grinned. 'More stock to deal with.'

'Indeed,' said Jemma. 'More for us too, I hope. I've got a list for him.'

'Another one?' asked Maddy. 'Didn't you go out yourself only a fortnight ago?'

'I refer you to Brian's observation, Maddy,' said Jemma. 'The books do seem to sell themselves.' She unhooked her jacket. 'Before I go, do you need anything? You've had your lunch, haven't you?'

Maddy rolled her eyes. 'That was an hour ago, Jemma. I'll be fine.'

'I'm sure you will,' said Jemma. 'I've got my mobile switched on, so—'

'I'll be fine,' Maddy repeated. And in her heart of hearts, Jemma knew she would. The threat of her old boss, Brian, had been completely removed, but it was hard not to worry. Even more so when you were the proprietor of the bookshop.

'If we don't go soon the shop will be closed,' said Luke, and opened the door. Jemma realised with a start that he hadn't put his sunglasses on, as he usually did when leaving the shop. Then again, the sky was dull, uniform grey, with no sun to be seen. Luke would be perfectly safe.

They arrived at Burns Books a minute later to find Raphael patting his pockets. 'I know I left them somewhere…'

'Do you mean these?' said Jemma, pointing at a set of keys dangling from a hook behind the counter. To do so she had to lean around Folio, who was sitting on a stack of paper bags on the counter, making a pleasing swish with every movement of his tail. 'You won't get far without Gertrude.'

'Don't I know it,' said Raphael.

'Meow,' put in Folio, and Jemma scratched him behind the ears, which elicited a loud purr.

'All OK at the shop?' she asked.

'Of course,' said Raphael. 'Another busy morning, just how we like it.'

'Any thoughts on the Christmas window display? Ours has got a mantelpiece with stockings and a tree and book presents.'

'Has it, now?' Raphael glanced at the window, which was currently full of Scots-themed books for St Andrew's Day. 'Well, as long as there's not too much for Folio to scramble up and knock over, you may do as you wish.'

'No Christmas trees then, I take it,' said Jemma, and Folio thumped his tail in a way that suggested he would get the better of any tree that entered the shop. 'Oh yes.' She reached into her pocket and handed Raphael a sheet of paper.

He opened it, and whistled. 'That's quite a list,' he said.

3

'I know,' said Jemma. 'I'm guessing lots of people will come in with ten or fifteen or twenty pounds to spend on someone. I want books which feel like a treat, but won't break the bank.' Her book-buying policy was about as different from Brian's as could be.

Raphael looked impressed. 'A sound strategy,' he said. 'Whereas I buy whatever calls to me.'

Jemma made a face. 'Don't bring back anything too feisty this time, will you?' On Raphael's last expedition he had brought back an annotated copy of *Daemonologie* which had been so volatile that they had had to put it in a lead-lined box. Luckily Raphael had sold it two days later to a collector, but Jemma still wondered sometimes what had become of the book, or the collector.

'Well, standing here talking won't get books bought,' said Raphael. He unhooked the keys, then tossed them in the air and caught them, to Folio's intense interest. 'To the camper van!' He picked up a stack of flat boxes and strode away, whistling.

'Right,' said Jemma, taking off her jacket and rubbing her hands. 'I'll go and see what's happening downstairs, get a coffee, then have a think about the window.' She glanced at Luke. 'Do you want anything?'

Luke grinned, showing his long canines. 'Maybe a decaf tea,' he said. 'I ate earlier.' Jemma thought of the opaque Tupperware boxes which Luke brought in with him, and did her best not to grimace.

Downstairs, in the restored crypt which formed the main part of the bookshop, the café was busier than the bookshelves, though perhaps fifteen or twenty people were

4

browsing, almost all with a book or two in their hand. Jemma waved to Carl, who was serving a customer. The seating area was half full, and Jemma suspected there would be another surge of customers when school finished for the day.

She strolled around the shop, occasionally re-shelving a book that had been left on a table, or turning one that had been put the wrong way up. Most of their customers were careful and neat, but even so, the books often rearranged themselves. 'I'll come back,' she mouthed to Carl, but he was busy with the next customer and didn't see. *It doesn't matter,* she thought. *I'll see him later. Maybe we can go for a drink, or have a coffee together after we've closed.*

Jemma went upstairs, stood outside the shop and looked at the window. It was a shame she couldn't do the same display here, but they couldn't have two identical windows within a hundred metres, and she dreaded to think what Folio would do to it. But it would be nice to have a display he could interact with… A thought came to her, and she went inside and rummaged in the stockroom.

'Are we running low on books downstairs?' called Luke.

'Not exactly,' Jemma called back, then emerged with two large cardboard boxes. 'I've had an idea.' She put the boxes by the window. 'I'm nipping over to mine. I won't be a moment.'

Luke cast his eyes to the heavens as she left. He goggled at her when she returned with a bundle of white sheets in her arms. 'You're decorating for Christmas, not Halloween.'

5

'Wait and see,' said Jemma, and vanished into the window. An hour later, after various trips downstairs, into the stockroom, and further afield, she beckoned to him. 'You can look now.' She followed Luke outside.

Luke's jaw dropped, then he laughed. 'A snow scene!'

Jemma surveyed her work with pride. The sheets had become snow-covered ground, the display shelves were snowdrifts topped with books, and large sturdy twigs, windfalls from a nearby park, were strung with baubles. A beanbag and a cushion had been transformed into a plump snowman using a sheet, button eyes, a woollen scarf, and one of Raphael's hats, and a sled piled with books stood in the middle. But perhaps the best part was the white polystyrene packing beads all over the floor. Folio appeared from nowhere and dived into the middle of them, rolling and wriggling like a cat in clover.

'Oh, look at the cat!' said a passerby, pointing, and after watching Folio for a few seconds, she entered the shop.

Jemma and Luke exchanged glances. 'My work here is done,' said Jemma.

'Oh no it isn't,' said Luke. 'Customers.'

And he was right. When they re-entered the shop browsers had become purchasers, and a queue was forming at the counter. 'I'll go on the downstairs till,' said Jemma, 'or you'll be inundated.'

Luke eyed the queue, which was ten people long now. 'Indeed,' he said. 'Can't have that happening.' But he said it with a smile.

Jemma hurried down and installed herself behind the shop counter, and for the next half hour she barely had time to breathe as she rang up sale after sale. When it quietened, she noticed the Regency section of the romance shelves was rather bare, as was dystopian fiction. One of the things that pleased her about working in the bookshop was the unpredictability. *You just can't tell what will sell on any given day*, she reflected, as she ran upstairs to the stockroom.

Perhaps the worst thing was being so near the café and yet so far. Occasionally she cast an imploring glance at Carl, and sometimes she caught him looking at her, but he was still busy serving and she was trapped behind the counter. She wondered whether Raphael would be back before closing time, but suspected not; once he got talking about books to Dave Huddart, to name but one bookseller, all thoughts of time flew out of his head. She resigned herself to waiting until five o'clock for a drink.

But eventually the queue lessened, Jemma called the bookshop equivalent of time, and rang up her last sale. The café had closed at a quarter to five, and Carl was wiping tables. 'I'll just cash up and check on Luke,' Jemma called. 'And then I could murder a coffee, if the machine's still on.' Carl looked up and nodded, but said nothing.

Once the till takings had been counted, bagged, and locked away in the back-room safe, Jemma waved Luke off, secured the shop door, and headed downstairs. 'What a day,' she said, and smiled at Carl, who was sitting at one of the tables. He had a black coffee, and a cappuccino waited at the place opposite him.

Jemma walked over and put her hand on his shoulder, as she always did when she leaned down to kiss him—

'Jemma, I need to tell you something.'

Jemma couldn't make out Carl's expression. It didn't look like a terrible something, but he definitely wasn't comfortable.

She sat opposite him and sipped her cappuccino. 'Go on.'

He shifted slightly in his chair. 'You know everything's been . . . busy lately, what with the play, and that profile in the paper, and all the other stuff—'

Jemma smiled. 'I do. I've barely seen you.'

He smiled too, briefly. 'It's been ridiculous. Today I had two more calls, about a writer-in-residence thing and a mentoring scheme.'

Jemma reached for his hand. 'That's amazing!'

His mouth twitched. 'I missed both calls because of the lunch rush. I picked up the voicemails later, and I'll have to call them both back. The thing is, Jemma, there's so much going on, and I can't handle it.'

He met her eyes. 'I wanted to tell you earlier, but one or other of us has been busy all day. I haven't told anybody else yet, Jemma, but I'm leaving the shop. I'm handing in my notice tomorrow.'

Chapter 2

The lights overhead dimmed. 'Oh no,' murmured Jemma. 'It's all right,' she called. 'Don't worry.'

Suddenly it seemed cold. Jemma rubbed her arms, and wished she hadn't left her jacket upstairs. Even her feet were shivering – no, that wasn't it. The floor was trembling. 'Please don't do this,' she said, and heard the panic in her voice.

Carl looked stricken. 'I don't want to, Jemma, but—'

'I'm not talking to you!' she cried. 'I meant the shop!' She jumped as a book crashed onto the floor.

'Of course you did,' he said, and his tone was hard to read. He stood up, and gazed at the shelves and the flickering lights. 'It isn't you,' he said, his voice carrying to the end of the shop. 'It's me. It isn't your fault.'

The flickering stopped, as if the shop were listening.

'I have to go and do other things for a while.

9

They're . . . they're kind of bookish things.' Carl paused, judging the effect. 'Remember that play we did here? Maybe one day, if it all goes well, they'll make a book of it. If they do, I'll bring you a copy. I'll put it on the shelf. Right way up and everything.'

Jemma breathed out, and it felt as if the shop did too. There was an indefinable change in the atmosphere, as if a threatening storm had passed over.

'I doubt I'll be gone too long, anyway,' said Carl. 'It probably won't last.'

Jemma gave him a pained glance. 'Don't say that.'

'How do I know?' Carl spread his hands. 'Maybe I got lucky, those first two nights here. Maybe the play will bomb in a new venue. But I have to at least try.'

'I know you do,' said Jemma. 'But we'll miss you. I'll miss you.' She wanted to say, 'It won't be the same without you,' but she couldn't risk the shop hearing.

Carl smiled. 'I'm not breaking up with you!' He looked upwards. 'Or you.' For the first time, he seemed hopeful. 'If anything, I might have a bit more spare time. Not at first, not while we're rehearsing at the theatre and doing that first run. Not that it even *is* a theatre yet—'

'How's the refurbishment going?' asked Jemma.

'They're opening mid-December, and Rumpus is doing the first run, up to Christmas,' said Carl. 'No pressure whatsoever.'

Things had moved quickly after Carl's first play, *A New Leaf*, had premiered in the basement of Burns Books the previous month. The drama critic of the *Evening Clarion*, Henry Sims, had given the play a glowing review, which had led to Carl being included in a profile of up-and-coming creatives. Then Henry had told Carl about a community arts centre opening nearby which was seeking new plays to put on, and the rest, as they say, was history. Only history to be made.

'Exciting times,' said Jemma. *And for me too*, she thought, *getting a new barista settled in before Christmas.* 'Look, do you want to come back to mine? You've got calls to make, and it will be quiet.' Carl's face, which had been guarded, apprehensive, broke into a smile. 'I could cook for us both.'

His grin was like sunshine. 'I hoped you'd say that.'

Jemma got up and held her hand out to him. 'Come on.'

Carl took her hand and squeezed it, then picked up their cups, took them behind the counter and stacked them in the dishwasher.

'Always so tidy,' said Jemma, smiling. *How can I ever replace you?* Carl, who had helped her scrub the crypt clean when they were first getting ready to open it to the public. Who came in early and usually left late. Who worked through his breaks more often than not. She sighed. *Best not to think about this now. Not here.* She didn't think the shop could read her mind, but she could never be sure.

In the stillness of the shop, they heard the bell ring upstairs. 'That must be Raphael coming back,' said Jemma. A chill went through her all over again. *I can't face telling him yet.*

'Hello?' called Raphael. 'Anyone home?'

She glanced at Carl, who looked as uncomfortable as

11

she felt. 'Would you mind if we didn't tell him tonight?' he said. 'I ought to tell Giulia first. She's my real boss, even if I only pop into Rolando's to collect stuff these days. And she took me on when I was desperate for work.'

Relief washed over Jemma. 'I'm so glad you said that,' she muttered. 'Let's go up.' She made for the heavy oak door that led to the stairs. 'Carl and I were just leaving,' she called.

'I'll do final checks here and switch off the lights,' said Carl as she hurried away, 'then I'll follow you up.'

Upstairs, two cardboard boxes were sitting on the counter. The shop bell rang again, and Raphael came through the door carrying two more. 'Gertrude's outside,' he said, setting the boxes on the counter. 'I doubt the parking police will bother us.'

'A good haul, then?' said Jemma.

'Fifteen boxes,' said Raphael. 'Ten for me, five for you.' He patted the top of one. 'Do you want me to pick your boxes out? Then you can take them back to the shop with you.'

'No, it's fine,' said Jemma quickly. 'We can sort it in the morning.' The last thing she had in mind was for the shop to tell Raphael while she was there by putting *Tips For The Inexperienced Recruiter* or *Skills Every Young Barista Should Know* at the top of every box he opened.

Raphael looked at her, eyebrows raised. 'Are you sure, Jemma? It's unlike you not to dive into a new box of books.'

'I'm just a bit tired,' said Jemma. 'It's been a busy afternoon. Oh, I did the window, by the way. Not that you can see it in the dark…' She heard Carl's footsteps on the stairs. 'Why don't we help you get the rest of the boxes in, and then you can put Gertrude to bed. I imagine Folio wants his dinner.'

'Is it me,' said Raphael, 'or is it cold in here?' He scrutinised her. 'Are you sure everything's all right, Jemma?' He frowned. 'Where is Folio, anyway?'

A cross meow answered him, and Folio stalked in from the back room, tail sticking up, yellow eyes glaring. He stopped in front of Raphael and meowed again.

'Oh dear,' said Raphael, patting him carefully on the head. 'Someone's grumpy. Did I stay out too long?'

Folio turned his head away in apparent disgust.

'Maybe he's tired, too,' said Jemma. 'He was playing in the window display earlier. Don't worry, it's cat-friendly.'

'Were you now?' Raphael asked the cat, administering a long stroke to Folio's back and tail. 'In that case, I shall feed you as soon as I've got these books in. Yes, I shall.' Folio uttered a short sharp meow, jumped onto the counter, and nuzzled the corner of the nearest box. 'He's curious about them, even if you aren't,' Raphael remarked.

Fifteen minutes later the boxes were in, Gertrude the camper van had been dropped at her garage round the corner, and Jemma and Carl took their leave. 'Doing anything nice?' Raphael enquired.

'Just a quiet meal together,' said Jemma, hoping she didn't look as guilty and furtive as she felt. 'See you tomorrow.'

'Indeed,' said Raphael. He bent down. 'Now, Folio, would you prefer chicken or tuna?'

Jemma and Carl walked slowly along the road. It was mild weather for December; the blanket of cloud was at least good for something. 'It's not as if I'm the only barista in the world,' Carl said, apropos of nothing. 'I'm not even very good. Not like the ones who do fancy patterns on top of their coffee.'

Jemma slipped her hand into his. 'But you're our barista.' She paused. 'Well, you were.'

He looked at her with a tight smile. 'Still am, for now. I have to give a week's notice.' He eyed the brightly lit shop windows all around them, then shrugged. 'I'll probably be back in January, anyway. That's if you'll have me.' And then Jemma knew that while she would miss Carl, she really, really wanted him to succeed.

'You won't. It'll be brilliant, wait and see.' She squeezed his hand, then quickened her pace. 'Maddy will have closed up, but I'll need to check the shop and make sure the cash is put away. You can return those phone calls while I do that and decide what to cook.'

'Yes, boss.' Carl aimed a playful punch at her arm, then both their expressions changed as they realised that was probably the last time he would call her that, even in play. *It's a good thing*, Jemma told herself as she unlocked the door of The Friendly Bookshop and switched the lights on. *It's a weird situation anyway, managing someone you go out with. And it's a great chance for Carl. I can't be selfish about this.* But despite all her self-talk, Jemma felt a pang at the thought that one day soon, she would walk downstairs at Burns Books and not find him there.

Chapter 3

The next morning, Jemma waited for Maddy to arrive with some trepidation. On one hand, by the time she arrived at Burns Books Carl would already have told Raphael his news. On the other, she suspected that through the machinations of the shop, Raphael would already know, and quite possibly be angry with them both.

She was pondering this pleasing conundrum and resigning herself to getting the blame either way when the shop bell rang. 'You're early,' she said to Maddy.

'Yes,' said Maddy, hanging up her jacket and tote bag. 'It's Tuesday.' Jemma looked blank. 'Stocktake day. Remember? We brought it forward because of Christmas.'

'Of course it is,' said Jemma. 'I completely forgot. Although actually I'll be bringing new stock back from Burns Books this morning.'

'Oh,' said Maddy, various expressions flitting over her

face as she processed this information. 'In that case, shall I leave the stocktake until this afternoon?'

'What a good idea,' said Jemma. If things didn't go well at Burns Books this morning, at least she could take refuge in serving the customers while Maddy updated the stock database and arranged the stockroom. She got up and collected her own jacket and bag. 'I'd better go there now. Maybe I can sort the books out and bring them back before we open.' *Yes, that's a good way to keep things brief. I can take my reprimand and go.*

She fully expected to be glared at by both Raphael and Folio when she arrived at Burns Books. However, Raphael was sitting in the armchair, spectacles on the end of his nose and deep in a book, with Folio dozing on his lap. 'Ah, good morning Jemma,' he said. 'Your books are outside the stockroom door.'

'Oh,' said Jemma. 'Good. I'll just, um, collect those and be on my way, if you don't mind me borrowing the trolley.'

Raphael put his book face down on his lap. 'Could we have a quick chat first?'

'Of course,' said Jemma. She glanced at the book: *Managing Your Team.* Her stomach lurched. 'About anything in particular?'

'Well, yes,' said Raphael.

Jemma braced herself and racked her brain for placatory phrases.

'Now, you haven't been in post at The Friendly Bookshop for long, and it must be difficult managing things across two bookshops, especially with Christmas coming.' Raphael pushed his glasses up and looked through them at her. 'However, there are certain things I would like you to consider picking up.'

Jemma goggled at him, her brain working furiously. Was it possible that Carl hadn't given notice yet? And what could Raphael mean? 'I'm sorry,' she said eventually, 'but I don't understand.'

'Your duties as Assistant Keeper,' said Raphael. 'You're doing a great job working across this bookshop and your own, but we mustn't lose sight of the wider scope of your role.'

'Oh,' said Jemma. 'I see. Maybe after Christmas—'

'I don't think it can wait that long,' said Raphael, and while he said it calmly, Jemma knew there was no point in arguing.

'I don't feel ready,' she said, thinking of the job description which she had helped to draw up a few short weeks ago, never dreaming she would have to fulfil it.

Raphael laughed. 'There is no ready,' he said. 'You just get on and do it. I'm not proposing to make you do everything at once. I mean, I wouldn't expect you to handle a full-scale knowledge emergency on your own.'

Jemma shuddered. 'Good.' For a moment, a picture of fleeing customers in a dark bookshop and a shelf of glowing, juddering books filled her mind. She blinked and focused on Folio lying curled on Raphael's lap, his usual sleek self. 'What do you have in mind?'

Raphael reached into his jacket pocket and extracted a folded piece of paper. 'Apart from the knowledge emergency aspect of the role, which I've already said I don't expect you to handle yet, there are several other responsibilities of a less – alarming nature.'

I'll be the judge of that, thought Jemma.

Raphael unfolded the sheet. 'Visiting principal bookshops, libraries, and other book repositories in the area of jurisdiction,' he read, 'and forming relationships with the managers thereof.' He looked over his glasses at Jemma. 'That means having coffee with local contacts and chatting about books.' He smiled. 'Pastries are optional.'

'Oh yes,' said Jemma, 'I can do that.'

'Excellent,' said Raphael. He produced a pencil and ticked an item. 'Then we have a list of committees and subcommittees which Brian either served on or chaired. I don't expect you to take them on all at once, but I would like you to attend two and chair one.'

Jemma swallowed. 'But I don't know very much.'

'You'll learn,' said Raphael. 'Besides, aren't you always talking about getting more representation from people outside the traditional sphere of Keepers? Now is your chance to be that representation.'

'It's rather mean of you to use my own arguments against me,' said Jemma.

'Perhaps you should be proud that I've learned from you,' said Raphael. Folio stretched out a lazy paw and yawned.

'OK,' said Jemma. 'I presume you have a list.'

'Of course,' said Raphael, waving his piece of paper. 'I'll read, you choose. Although there is one in particular I would like you to take on.' He cleared his throat and held the paper at arm's length. 'Subcommittee for the

Consideration of Antiquarian Bindings.'

'No,' said Jemma.

'Ancient Greek and Sanskrit Study Group.'

'Absolutely not,' said Jemma, laughing.

'Committee for the Approval of New Translations of Works of Classical Antiquity.'

Jemma shook her head. 'I wouldn't have a clue.'

'To be honest, I'm planning to wind that group up,' said Raphael. 'They never approve any new translations, and it doesn't really matter if they do. I think the last one they let through was George Chapman's Homer.' He ran his finger down the list. 'Ah, here's one you might like; it's a discussion group. The Novel: Friend or Foe?'

Jemma bit her lip. 'I'm guessing that's quite a negative group.'

'You could turn it around,' said Raphael.

'OK,' said Jemma. 'Put me down for that. But I don't want to chair it.'

The corner of Raphael's mouth curled up. 'I'll give it three months until you do,' he said. 'Oh yes, and this one has your name written all over it. Management Strategies for Keepers. That's an interesting group with a varied membership, and with your skills you'd be perfect.' He eyed her. 'Brian chaired it.'

Jemma stared at her boss. 'Brian? But he hypnotised his assistant, and blackmailed Luke, and—'

'And you can advocate less coercive methods of keeping one's staff and associates in line.'

Jemma drew herself up. *At last, something I actually know about.* 'All right then,' she said, 'I will. Put me down for chair.'

'Wonderful!' Raphael ticked the paper. 'You'll have the chance to talk to people all over the country. Some you won't know, of course, but a few you've met already: Nina, Percy, Drusilla…'

'Wait a minute,' said Jemma. 'Drusilla's in the group?'

'Naturally,' said Raphael. 'She owns a large and successful bookshop in Windsor.'

'And she despises me,' said Jemma. 'I can't chair a group with her in it.'

'Oh, Drusilla despises everyone,' said Raphael. 'You'll get used to it.'

'I won't,' said Jemma. 'I'll chair another group instead. I'll attend that group if you want, but rub out the chair bit.'

Raphael held up his pencil. 'Sorry,' he said. 'No rubber.'

Jemma gave him a hard stare, 'Just cross it out, then.'

'Ah, but it's not as easy as that,' said Raphael. 'It's a Pencil of Truth, you see. I can't do that without explaining. Anyway, you're the best person to do that.' He held out the pencil and paper. 'Here you go. Write down why you can't chair that meeting.'

Jemma's brain churned with all the things she wanted to say on the subject of why she couldn't chair that meeting. Frankly, a ream of paper wouldn't be enough. But admitting it… She lifted her chin. 'Fine,' she said. 'I'll chair one meeting. But if I don't like it—'

'I understand,' said Raphael. 'Actually, they're due a meeting soon. Have a look in the shop diary and see if you can fit one in before Christmas. All done virtually, of course. And since you've agreed to that one, how about a place on the social committee? It isn't one of Brian's, but Nina is very nice and she'd welcome the help. The Christmas do is already organised, of course.'

Jemma shrugged. 'Why not.'

Raphael ticked the list, then scrutinised her. 'Oh dear,' he said. 'Are you really worried about Drusilla?'

Jemma sighed. 'Partly that, but—' She swallowed. 'I thought you wanted to talk about something else. This is quite a surprise.'

'Ah,' said Raphael. 'Carl leaving, I presume?' He smiled at her expression. 'The shop let me know about that last night.' He tapped *Managing Your Team*. 'It's perfectly natural that he wants to follow his dream. To be honest, I was surprised he left it so long.'

'So you don't mind?'

'No,' said Raphael. 'Giulia will ask among her staff if anyone would like to move over to the bookshop, and if not, we'll recruit someone. When you've run a business for as long as I have, you don't worry so much about staff moving on. Although of course I wouldn't want to lose any of you,' he added hastily. 'Perhaps we could invite Carl back for an author event.'

'Oh yes, that's a great idea,' said Jemma. Behind her, the letterbox rattled. 'Post's early,' she said. 'Oh, just a flyer.' She passed it to Raphael without looking at it.

'We are seeking properties in your area,' he read. 'Best prices paid. Speedy resolution.' He crumpled it into a ball, aimed at the bin, and missed. Folio sat straight up, then leapt after it. 'Ow!' cried Raphael. 'Claws, Folio!'

21

'Do you ever get tired of running the shop?' asked Jemma. 'I mean, you've been doing it for . . . how long?'

'A couple of hundred years, in this shop,' said Raphael, watching Folio pick up the ball of paper in his mouth, drop it, then bat it under a shelf. 'No, not really. Always new books to read, of course.' He tapped the book on his lap, which had become *Ready Player Two*. 'Oh, Folio.' The cat was standing by the door, hackles raised and tail straight up, yowling to be let out. 'Could you open the door for him, Jemma?'

'Is he allowed on the main road?'

'He'll be fine,' said Raphael. 'I pity the car that tries to run him over.'

'Be careful,' Jemma told Folio, and opened the door. He whisked through and trotted off, a cat on a mission. 'Was there anything else?' she asked Raphael. 'If not, I should probably take my books and head back. It's stocktake day, and you know how Maddy is.'

'Oh, I do.' They exchanged glances. Maddy had mellowed considerably since Brian's departure, but she was still a stickler for some things. 'I'll send you information on those committees. We can settle up for the books later.'

'Can't wait,' said Jemma, with a grimace, and went to fetch the bookshop trolley.

Ten minutes later, armed with a takeaway cappuccino from downstairs, she was wheeling her haul to The Friendly Bookshop, feeling as if she had done a day's work already. The crisis she had expected hadn't happened, but a whole new world of antagonism and red tape awaited her.

On balance, she thought, a large-scale knowledge emergency would have been easier to manage.

Chapter 4

'You were quick,' said Maddy, as Jemma wheeled the trolley into The Friendly Bookshop. Jemma got the impression that she was cross at being disturbed.

'Yes, I was, wasn't I,' said Jemma, without enthusiasm. 'How's it going?'

'Oh, fine,' said Maddy, waving a hand. 'No problems, everything under control. What have you got here?'

'I haven't looked yet,' said Jemma. 'I just brought the boxes back.'

Maddy peered at her. 'Are you all right?'

Jemma shrugged. 'More responsibilities.' Then she glanced at Maddy and cursed her stupidity. Of course! Maddy, more than anyone, would know how Brian had managed things. 'Do you know anything about Brian's various committees?'

Maddy considered, her slender hands resting on the

topmost box. 'He thought them very important. He used to say that an organisation was controlled through its committees, and that a word in the right place could lead to the fall of an empire.'

Jemma shivered. 'That sounds about right.'

'But as for detail… No, not really. He tended to make cryptic comments about the committees rather than tell me what went on in them.' She glanced at Jemma. 'Is that what Raphael wants you to do, join committees?'

'Yes,' said Jemma. 'And chair one. A scary one.'

'Oh, you'll be fine,' said Maddy. 'One thing Brian did say was that it was always best to chair a meeting because then you give the actions to everyone else.'

'Knowing my luck, they'll refuse,' said Jemma gloomily. 'Let's get these books unpacked; that might take my mind off it.'

But somehow not even the pleasurable process of lifting books out of their boxes, piling them on the counter, trying them in different places in the shop, and entering them on the database could remove the nagging doubt from Jemma's mind. *I should just get on with it*, she thought. *The more worrying I do, the worse I'll feel. Besides, I can't do much until Raphael sends over the information he promised.*

Her phone pinged, and she grimaced. Luckily, she was saved from having to open the email by the entrance of a customer looking for something very particular. 'The book was definitely blue,' she said. 'No, not that blue. Dark blue. And the writing on it was white. Or maybe yellow.'

'Can you remember what it was about?' asked Jemma.

25

'Was it a novel? A recent book?'

'I think there were clouds on the front,' said the customer, gripping her elbows.

After ten minutes of pulling out this book and that book, the customer finally gave a yelp of recognition at a dark-red book with an abstract cover. 'That's the one!' she said, with a pleased expression. 'I was sure I would know it when I saw it.'

'Glad to be of service,' said Jemma. 'Would you like a bag?'

While Maddy shelved the rest of the books, Jemma alternated between serving customers and looking through a directory of libraries and bookshops in Westminster. *Presumably I don't have to have coffee in every single one*, she thought. *The Westminster bit of Charing Cross Road alone would take some time. Then the London Library, Westminster Reference Library, Marylebone Library, Mayfair Library... Do I go to the chain bookstores? Perhaps I should let them know I'm here...*

She remembered when she had first come to work at Burns Books, and had been mystified by the amount of 'just popping out' that Raphael did, and how often he returned from those expeditions with a coffee cup or a paper bag from Rolando's. *He's probably a significant income stream for that shop.* Then again, since he seemed completely unaffected by either caffeine or eating multiple pastries every day, why not? *I wonder if I'll be the same. After all, I'm an Assistant Keeper. Imagine being able to eat and drink whatever I wanted and not gain weight or feel ill—*

'Hello?' Luke waved a hand in front of her face. 'Are you having a nice dream?'

'I was thinking about work,' said Jemma, with dignity.

'If you were anyone else, Jemma,' he replied, 'I'd say that no one looks that pleased about work.'

'How come you're here so early?' asked Jemma.

'I'm not,' said Luke. 'I've come to take Maddy to lunch.'

Jemma glanced at the grandfather clock in the corner. 'Good grief, where has the morning gone?'

'Time flies when you're having fun,' said Luke, and winked. 'Back in an hour.'

Jemma watched them go. It was lovely to see Luke and Maddy's relationship blossoming, and it made sense for him to take advantage of the darker winter days… But it also made her examine the brief snatches of time that she and Carl currently spent together. They could never go for lunch at the same time, for instance, and more often than not, when he was finished in the café and had spare time before rehearsals with his theatre company, Rumpus, she was cashing up or planning for the next day in the shops.

Jemma was still lost in a reverie of how unfair things sometimes were when the shop telephone rang. 'Good afternoon, The Friendly Bookshop,' she said, trying to put a smile in her voice.

'Someone sounds cheerful,' said Raphael. 'Are you pleased with your books?'

'Of course,' said Jemma, 'they're lovely. Thank you. I couldn't have made a better selection myself.'

'Yes, well,' said Raphael. 'I don't suppose Folio's over

27

there, is he?'

'No, I haven't seen him,' said Jemma, craning her neck to look around the shop. 'Hasn't he come back?'

'Not yet,' said Raphael. 'I'm sure he's fine, but… Tell me if you see him.'

'I shall,' said Jemma. 'Was that all you rang for?'

'I sent you an email,' said Raphael. 'I don't know if you've opened it, but—'

'Not yet,' said Jemma. 'We've been busy in the shop.'

'Oh good,' said Raphael. 'I thought you'd probably prefer more information rather than less, but you don't need to read all of it.'

'When you say all of it…' Jemma grabbed her mobile from the counter and opened the email app. The message at the top was titled *Committee Information*. She clicked on it. 'Fifty-nine attachments?'

'I know you like to be thorough,' said Raphael, sounding guilty, 'but that doesn't mean you should read every word.'

'*Fifty-nine?*' Jemma wailed.

'That's the last year's worth of committee minutes plus other documents: membership list, remit of the committee, any reports or papers… One of them has a mission statement; shall I send that too?'

'No,' said Jemma. 'Thank you. I'll make do with what I have.' *Perhaps it's as well I'm not going out with Carl every night*, she thought bitterly. *I wouldn't have time.*

'Oh, and one other thing,' said Raphael. 'Giulia popped over earlier and none of her staff want to come and work at the bookshop. They're happy where they are, so we'll have to recruit from outside.'

'Oh great,' said Jemma. 'That's just wonderful.'

'Yes,' said Raphael. 'We'll be able to pick someone who understands books as well as beverages, hopefully. It must be a joint interview – while the new barista will be with us full-time, Giulia will still be their boss – but we can cross that bridge when we come to it. Perhaps Carl can be on the interview team. He knows our little foibles, and it would be good to have an independent view.'

'That's if we can get anybody this close to Christmas,' said Jemma.

'And why wouldn't we?' asked Raphael. 'A pleasant workplace, friendly colleagues, staff discounts, even a resident cat . . . when he turns up.'

'When does Carl finish?' asked Jemma. *At this rate I'll be working the coffee machine. Heaven help the customers.*

'Officially, in a week's time,' said Raphael. 'However, he's offered to stay on a bit longer if needed so that the new barista can shadow him.'

'OK,' said Jemma. 'We'd better get a move on, then.'

'Never fear,' said Raphael, 'Giulia has already placed an advert.'

'Oh,' said Jemma. 'Good.'

'So there's nothing for you to worry about, Jemma,' said Raphael. 'Leave it to us. Oh, a customer. Speak to you later, maybe.'

'Yes, speak to you later,' echoed Jemma, and heard the dial tone as the receiver at the other end was plonked back on its cradle.

She stood for a while, looking at the phone. *Am I having a bad day? Or am I being more negative than usual?* Then, luckily, one of their regulars came in seeking a Dodie Smith book she hadn't read. Checking the shelves and the database kept Jemma pleasantly occupied for the next five minutes, and she was able to send the customer away with three new volumes and a smile.

Luke and Maddy erupted into the shop one minute before the hour was up – not that Jemma was keeping tabs, of course. 'Safely delivered on time,' said Luke.

Jemma gave him a withering glance. 'I wasn't counting.'

Luke and Maddy exchanged conspiratorial looks. 'No, of course not,' said Luke. 'See you later, Maddy.'

'I don't clock-watch,' said Jemma, as Maddy hung up her coat.

'I did see you peep when we came in,' said Maddy. 'We know when we're due back.'

'I know you do,' said Jemma. 'Would you mind if I popped out? I need to shop for dinner.' That wasn't exactly true. In her flat upstairs she had cupboards full of food, but right now something quick, easy and comforting was definitely on the menu for tonight, and besides, she could do with a change of scene.

Maddy shrugged. 'Sure,' she said. She inspected the fiction shelves and straightened a few books which had become disarranged. Thoroughly irritated, Jemma picked up her bag and sloped off.

It isn't their fault, she thought, as she walked to Nafisa's mini market. *I'm the manager of the shop and it's up to me*

30

to handle setbacks, not lean on my staff.

When she pushed open the door of the mini market, Nafisa was leaning on the counter, eating something which smelt delicious out of a Tupperware container, and reading the *Financial Times*. 'Hello there,' she said.

'Hi,' said Jemma, edging towards the display of ready meals. She shouldn't, but Nafisa's curry smelt so nice…

'You do know that's probably full of additives,' said Nafisa, as Jemma put the packet on the counter.

'I'll survive,' said Jemma. 'Not your usual reading matter,' she added, indicating the paper.

'I'm broadening my horizons,' said Nafisa. She closed the paper carefully, folded it, and put it back in the rack by the counter. 'Anything else? Diet Coke? Peppermint Aero?'

'Please don't tempt me,' said Jemma. 'I've got a nice healthy lunch waiting for me at the shop, and I really ought to eat it.' Then she caught sight of something half hidden by the impulse buys stacked at the edges of the counter. 'We got one of those flyers too.'

'I imagine everyone did,' said Nafisa. 'I rang the number to see what they're offering and it isn't bad at all. Over market value. Not that it's up to me, I only rent.'

'The owner wouldn't sell it without talking to you first, would they?' Jemma touched her phone to the card reader.

Nafisa shrugged. 'Who knows? But there's plenty of time left on my lease, so he'd have to do a little persuading.' She rubbed her thumb and forefinger together and grinned.

'You don't sound too upset about it,' said Jemma.

'Things happen,' said Nafisa. 'We'll see.' She leaned

31

towards the newspaper and magazine rack and selected *Property Week.* 'It never hurts to be prepared, though.'

'No, I suppose not,' said Jemma. 'Bye.' She picked up her ready meal and left, feeling thoroughly disconsolate. *All those courses I went on. All those change-management seminars and resilience sessions. And now change is here, I'm not handling it well at all.* She headed back to the shop and put her ready meal in the staff fridge, where it sat looking indigestible. *Things will get better*, she thought. *They must.*

Chapter 5

'What are you reading?' asked Maddy, peering at the cover of Jemma's book.

'*A Short History of the Novel*,' replied Jemma.

Maddy wrinkled her nose. 'Doesn't look short to me.' She gazed quizzically at Jemma. 'Is it interesting?'

Jemma closed the book on her finger. 'That depends on your definition of interesting. Anyway, it's necessary.'

'Is it?'

Jemma sighed. 'The Novel: Friend or Foe discussion group is meeting this Friday.'

'But you read loads of novels,' said Maddy. 'Do you need to know the history of the whole genre?'

'That's the problem – I don't know. And the shop's been so busy that I've hardly had any time to prepare.' As if on cue, the shop bell rang. 'See what I mean?' murmured Jemma. She slid a bookmark into the book and put it under the counter.

It had taken her most of the weekend to go through all the attachments Raphael had sent her. The minutes of the novel discussion group, to be fair, hadn't been so bad, though the summary of the discussion had revealed a breadth and depth to the members' knowledge which was, frankly, unsettling. *Maybe I can keep quiet*, she had thought. *But what if they ask me for my opinion?* On learning that the next meeting was coming up shortly, Jemma had panicked, gone round to Burns Books, and borrowed whatever she could find that might be useful. A small stack of books eyed her reproachfully whenever she reached under the counter for a paper bag. And as for the management group—

'You don't have to know everything,' said Maddy, once the customer had left with a bag full of books.

'That's good,' said Jemma, 'because I don't. But I don't want them to think I know nothing. Good morning,' she said automatically, as the shop bell rang again. 'How may I – oh! Hello, Giulia.'

'Ciao, Jemma,' said Giulia. 'We've closed the advert. Forty people applied.'

'Forty?'

'Yes,' said Giulia, glancing at the book in Jemma's hand. 'So I have some reading too. Unless I sell up, of course.' She laughed heartily.

'Have you had a flyer too?' asked Jemma. 'About selling the shop?'

Giulia executed a dramatic shrug. 'Hasn't everyone?' She smiled. 'I go to visit the bank manager now, but not

34

for that reason. Ciao.' She breezed out with the air of someone from whom problems slid away like water off a duck's back.

Jemma gazed at the door long after Giulia had gone through it. 'I wonder…'

Maddy looked at the clock, then her. 'Do you want to take an early lunch?'

Jemma considered. 'Do you know, I wouldn't mind.'

Forty minutes later she returned, ready to burst with news. 'That was interesting,' she said, hanging up her jacket.

'What was?' said Maddy. 'You picked the right time to go for lunch; I haven't stopped. Look at the shelves.' She waved her hand at the row facing them, which appeared decidedly gappy. 'I might as well not have bothered putting that new stock away; it will all have to come out.'

'I know,' said Jemma. 'And I'll help you. But listen a minute. Someone put a flyer through the door of Burns Books the other day, saying they wanted to buy properties.'

'I imagine that happens quite often,' said Maddy. 'They probably leafleted the whole street if they're looking in this area.'

'But we haven't had one, have we? We're only a hundred metres down the road, if that,' said Jemma.

Maddy shrugged. 'True.'

'Giulia's had one. And when I went to the mini market the other day, Nafisa had had one. So I went to the other shops in the parade, and they've had one too. James's Antique Emporium, Snacking Cross Road, Nafisa's, Rolando's, and the estate agents have all had a flyer, but

35

when I asked at the shops on either side of the parade, none of them had seen it. So somebody wants to buy up the parade. Including Burns Books.'

Maddy pursed her lips, thinking. 'They might want to,' she said, 'but that doesn't mean they'll be able to. Presumably everyone has to agree, and Raphael and Giulia won't. So I guess that's that.'

The grandfather clock struck the hour to confirm her statement.

Jemma exhaled, and smiled. 'You're right, Maddy. Of course you are.'

Maddy smiled back. 'I'm right, and I'm also off for lunch. Much as I love my job, I think an hour outside will do me good.' She eyed Jemma. 'You should have a proper break later, too. Dashing round on a flyer hunt isn't exactly restful.' And with that she shrugged on her jacket, slung her tote bag over her shoulder, and strolled out.

Jemma gazed after her. *Maybe I'm overthinking things.* She fetched her lunch from the fridge and flicked the kettle on.

Afterwards, she wondered whether switching on the kettle had been a sign to all the book buyers in Westminster to pay the shop a visit. When Maddy returned, Jemma had managed precisely two bites of her cream-cheese bagel, and the cup of tea remained unmade.

'Busy, I see,' Maddy remarked, eyeing the queue. 'Shall I get more stock out?'

'Please,' said Jemma. 'And more bags, if you could. And a new till roll.'

Maddy's eyes widened. 'On it,' she said, and scurried

off.

The pace slowed at two, but as it was good weather for December there were still enough browsers and buyers to keep things lively until around four o'clock. Apart from a five-minute tea break, when Jemma finally managed to eat the rest of her bagel, she and Maddy were kept busy on the tills or restocking.

'So this is the Christmas rush,' said Maddy. 'I haven't seen one of those for a while.'

'Will it be like this every day?' asked Jemma. 'Maybe I should start buying energy drinks.' She looked at the shelves which they had just replenished. There were still gaps here and there, but not half as many as in the stockroom.

'Who knows,' said Maddy. 'But you'll need to go book buying again. Most of those books you brought back the other day have gone already.'

'You're right. At this rate we'll have nothing left to sell in a couple of days.' Jemma fetched her phone and opened the calendar app. 'Friday's out, because of that meeting, and I'm usually at Burns Books on Thursday morning…' She looked up at Maddy. 'When would you say our quietest day is, normally?'

'Wednesday,' said Maddy, promptly.

'I agree,' said Jemma. 'And today's Monday.' She glanced at Maddy. 'Would you mind holding the fort? I can ask whether Luke could help.'

Maddy grinned. 'Oh, go on, then.'

'In that case,' said Jemma, 'I'll nip down and see if Gertrude is available.'

When she arrived at Burns Books, it was as busy as The Friendly Bookshop had been earlier. Luke was serving a line of customers, most of whom held a small pile of books. Perhaps he wouldn't be free to help Maddy after all.

'Is Raphael in?' Jemma asked.

'He's on the till downstairs,' said Luke. 'With Folio.'

'He's back, then?'

Luke grinned. 'Yes, and grounded. I think he's had a bit of an adventure.'

Jemma found Raphael dealing with a longer queue downstairs. Folio was sitting on the edge of the counter furthest from the customers, looking mutinous, and Jemma noticed a small bald patch on the back of his left ear. 'Have you been in the wars?' she asked, but Folio turned his head away.

'I suspect someone has been scrapping with another cat,' said Raphael. 'That's sixteen pounds ninety-five, please, madam.'

Jemma frowned. 'That's not like him.'

'No, it isn't,' said Raphael. 'Particularly as Folio is, well, immune to most attacks. So I'm wondering how on earth he's managed to pick up an injury.'

Folio glared at them both.

'You silly cat,' said Jemma, stroking him. 'Shall I get you an espresso, Raphael?'

'Would you mind?' said Raphael. 'I think I need one.'

Jemma surveyed the café area. By a miracle there was no queue, but Carl was talking to a dark-haired woman in jeans and a denim jacket. Even from behind she was stylish, and somehow she seemed familiar. Jemma

38

wandered over, but when she was about twenty feet away a small group of customers cut across her path, and when they dispersed the woman had vanished.

'Can I have an espresso for Raphael, please,' she said.

'Sure.' Carl got to work. He looked regretful as he set the small cup on the counter. 'It's weird to think I probably don't have many more of these left to do.'

'But nice too, I imagine,' said Jemma. 'Who were you chatting to?'

'A prospective replacement,' said Carl. 'She's coming to interview on Wednesday, so she popped in to see the place.'

'Wednesday?' said Jemma. 'So soon?'

'No time like the present,' said Carl.

Jemma delivered the espresso to Raphael. 'I hadn't realised you're interviewing for the new barista on Wednesday,' she said. 'I was about to ask if I could borrow Gertrude for a book-buying trip, but—'

'Go ahead,' said Raphael. 'There's already me, Giulia, and Carl on the panel, and we don't want to intimidate the poor things. At least, I suppose we shouldn't.'

'Oh,' said Jemma. 'If you're sure—' The thought of a solo trip in Gertrude, away from management responsibilities, was wonderful. 'Thanks. Let me know if there's anything you'd like me to look out for.'

'I think we're good for now,' said Raphael. 'If you come first thing on Wednesday you can take her then. I can spare Luke for the morning.'

'If you really don't mind,' said Jemma. She tried to distract herself from the idea that she was being got rid of.

'Oh, there was something else. You remember that flyer the other day? About selling the shop?'

Raphael glanced at her. 'Yes?'

'I did some digging in my lunch hour. Everyone in the parade got one, but no one did in the shops on either side.'

'Do excuse me a moment,' Raphael said to the next customer. 'Just in the parade?' he asked. 'You're sure?'

'Absolutely sure,' said Jemma. 'I checked five shops either way, to be on the safe side.'

'Hmm,' said Raphael. 'I don't like the sound of that.'

'Neither do I,' said Jemma. 'Although Maddy thinks nothing will come of it.'

'I hope she's right,' said Raphael. 'Though somehow I doubt it. Not that there's much we can do right now. Thank you for letting me know.' And he turned back to the customer.

So it isn't just me, thought Jemma, as she hurried to The Friendly Bookshop. *I'm definitely getting to the bottom of this.*

Chapter 6

Jemma walked down to Burns Books early on Wednesday morning, determined to enjoy herself. She had spent most of the evening before making a wish list of books to acquire. Some would complement her existing stock, some were replacements for titles which flew off the shelves, and some she just wanted to own, even for a short time.

The list had also helped to keep her mind off the fact that Carl was at yet another evening rehearsal. The new arts centre, though not ready to open, was safe enough for Rumpus to use the theatre space. 'It will give us such an advantage to get used to the stage good and early,' Carl had said, his eyes shining, and Jemma didn't have the heart to say the words buzzing round her head: *What about me? What about dinner? Or that drink we never get round to?*

Instead, she had nodded and said, 'Break a leg,' hoping she didn't sound as pathetic as she felt. But macaroni cheese, a glass of wine, a fresh sheet of her notebook, and a pen with sparkly purple ink had improved her mood considerably, though she felt that no bookshop on earth could possibly supply all her needs. Given Raphael's network of book dealers, though, it might just happen.

It's a beautiful crisp day, she thought. *I've got a flask of tea and a packed lunch, and I get to spend the day buying books. It doesn't get better than this.*

Jemma was surprised, when she got to the bookshop, to see that the lights were on; she had been fully prepared to let herself in and make conspicuous noise until Raphael finally made an appearance. She was even more surprised when she opened the door to find Raphael up, dressed, and having what sounded like a coherent conversation with another human being. 'Good morning, Jemma,' he said, as she closed the door behind her. 'Do you remember Mr Tennant?'

'From the Charing Cross branch of the Westminster Retailers' Association?' said Jemma, extending a hand, which he shook warmly. *Good heavens, I didn't expect to see him again until hell froze over.* 'How nice to see you, Mr Tennant.'

Mr Tennant beamed at her and waved his clipboard. 'I popped in because I need a venue for a meeting about the flyers that have been going round, and Mr Burns here has generously agreed to let us use the lower floor of the shop on Thursday evening.'

'Oh good,' said Jemma. 'I've been wondering about those flyers.'

Mr Tennant rocked on the balls of his feet, hugging the

clipboard to his chest as if it contained many secrets. 'You're not the only one, Jenny.'

'Jemma.'

'Oh yes,' he said. 'I've had quite a few people contact me, so I decided the best thing to do was to get everyone together and have it out. See what we all know.' He turned to Raphael. 'May I say, Mr Burns, how pleased I am to see you taking an interest in community affairs. You won't be sorry, I promise you.'

'I'm sure I won't,' Raphael replied. He closed his mouth firmly as soon as he finished speaking, and Jemma judged he was probably trying not to laugh. Still, it was a considerable advance from the rudeness Raphael had greeted Mr Tennant with the last time he had set foot in the shop.

'I'll get flyers printed up and distributed, then,' said Mr Tennant. 'Seven o'clock, Thursday evening, downstairs at Burns Books.' He eyed Raphael hopefully. 'Might there be refreshments?'

'Oh yes,' said Raphael. 'The attendees will need them.'

One in particular, thought Jemma.

'Wonderful,' said Mr Tennant. He consulted his clipboard, then took a pen from behind his ear and executed three ticks. 'I'll drop some in to you later today, if I may. To spread the word.' He nodded to them both, then strutted to the door. 'I'll see myself out,' he said, and was gone.

'What brought that on?' asked Jemma, once Raphael had finished chuckling.

Raphael straightened his bow tie and tugged down the

43

points of his waistcoat. 'Laziness, I'm afraid. I'd be interested to know what's behind those flyers, and if we meet here, I don't even have to step outside my front door. Plus the coffee will be good.' He leaned forward conspiratorially. 'It will be interesting to see who turns up.'

'Ooh,' said Jemma. 'I hadn't thought of that.'

Raphael tapped the side of his nose. 'You never know; getting on Tennant's good side could mean we get inside information.' A crafty smile played about his lips. 'Anyway,' he said, in a completely different tone, 'I suppose you want the keys to Gertrude. Where are you off to today?'

'The usual, I thought,' said Jemma. 'I'll start with Dave Huddart, and if Gertrude has any space left I might see what Elinor Dashwood has tucked away. I can always contact other people if I need to.' She held up her phone. 'Are you sure there's nothing you'd like me to look for?'

'Well, if you do see any seventeenth-century incunabula…' Raphael said thoughtfully, then laughed at her expression. 'Just focus on kitting out your own shop. Apart from anything else, what with barista interviews, this business with the flyers, and Mr Tennant's meeting tomorrow, I might need a little excursion of my own soon.' He paused. 'Do you have the essentials?'

'I think so,' said Jemma. 'Phone, purse, flask, packed lunch, list…' She waved the list at him. 'And you said there are boxes in Gertrude?'

'I did,' said Raphael. 'There's a first-aid kit in the glove box. As I haven't asked you to pick up anything for me, I doubt you'll require the chainmail gloves or the lead-lined box. Or the tongs.' He thought for a moment. 'Just in case…' He picked up a pencil from the counter and presented it to her. 'Ready-sharpened.'

'Pencil of Truth?' asked Jemma.

'Oh yes,' said Raphael. 'You can never be too careful.' He took Gertrude's keys from their hook. 'Bye, Folio!'

'Is Folio feeling better?' asked Jemma, as they walked along the street and rounded the corner.

'Oh yes,' said Raphael. 'You'd never know he'd been in a scrap.' He mused. 'It's still a mystery, though.'

'Well, if you solve it, let me know,' said Jemma.

'Here we are,' said Raphael, pointing to a line of garages set back from the road. He strode towards the middle door, which was battered enough to suggest it had been broken into several times, unlocked it, and lifted the door up and over to reveal Gertrude, gleaming in the thin wintry light like a Seville orange. 'As usual, she's got half a tank of fuel.' He handed Jemma the keys.

'Thanks, Raphael,' said Jemma, opening Gertrude's door and getting in. 'I'll take good care of her. Do you need her back by any particular time?'

'Not really,' said Raphael. 'We have five candidates to interview this afternoon, so I doubt I'll be going for a spin.'

Jemma turned the key in the ignition and Gertrude responded with a throaty growl that meant business. 'She wants to be off.'

'She does.' Raphael moved back and Jemma drove the camper van carefully out. 'Safe travels,' he said, as she passed him.

As usual when she travelled in Gertrude, Jemma was amused by how quiet the roads were in central London and how the traffic lights were always green. *I've been ruined for any other vehicle*, she thought, patting Gertrude's steering wheel.

The drive to Putney was quick and uneventful. Dave Huddart came out to meet her. 'Didn't expect to see you again so soon,' he observed, to Gertrude. 'Or you,' he added, to Jemma.

'Business is good,' said Jemma.

'It must be,' he said. 'You and Raphael are keeping me on my toes. Come on in.'

He led her past gleaming brass candelabra, coat racks standing to attention, rows and rows of shining oil lamps that simply must have genies inside, and a cluster of opened umbrella frames that reminded her of giant spiders. 'Here you go,' he said, indicating an array of bookshelves which, to Jemma's eye, looked as laden as ever. 'I'll pop back in half an hour and see how you're doing. Brew?'

'Yes please,' said Jemma, putting down her armful of flatpack boxes with a happy sigh.

***

Elinor Dashwood waved from the doorway of her semi-detached house as Jemma flicked Gertrude's lights on and pulled away. It had been quite a day.

In the end she had spent well over an hour browsing Dave's bookshelves, going methodically through her list, ticking off books she had found, and adding others which she discovered in her perusal of the shelves. Settling a price and getting the books packed had added a good half hour. Jemma was wheeling her first trolley-load of boxes to the car when a tall blond man strode in clutching a large, shabby, black-bound book.

'Is the boss in, my dear?' he asked, his gaze darting around as if Dave might be perched on the shelf or hanging from a light fitting. 'I've got a very rare book to show him.'

'He is in,' said Jemma, 'but I'm a customer.'

'Of course you are!' he said kindly.

Dave emerged from his sanctum, wheeling a spare trolley. 'Sebastian,' he said without enthusiasm. 'What is it this time?'

'Genuine original King James Bible,' said Sebastian, patting his burden. 'I've got paperwork and everything. Signed confirmation of authenticity.'

'By King James himself, I assume,' said Dave.

'As good as,' said Sebastian, winking at Jemma.

'Let's have a look, then,' said Dave, waving Sebastian into his office. 'How did you come by it?'

'That would be telling,' said Sebastian. 'It is genuine, though, I assure you.'

Dave examined the book carefully, handling it as if it were an unexploded bomb. 'It certainly looks the genuine article.'

'Could you sign a statement to that effect?' asked Jemma. 'Before you show us your paperwork.'

Sebastian drew himself up. 'I'd be delighted to.'

'Here you go.' Jemma pulled her battered, dogeared list from her pocket, spread it blank side down on the desk, and retrieved the Pencil of Truth from her bag. 'Something like "The book I have brought in today is a genuine

47

original King James Bible.'" She handed him the pencil.

Sebastian eyed it with disdain. 'I have a perfectly good fountain pen with me,' he said, producing one from his breast pocket. 'Such a statement should surely be written in ink.'

'Humour me,' said Jemma.

With a theatrical sigh, Sebastian bent to the task, his blond hair flopping over his eyes. 'The book I have brought in today,' he recited, writing in a looping hand, 'is a ge—'

The pencil lead broke.

Sebastian laughed. 'That's why we use pens.' He turned the pencil and attempted to continue, but he hadn't even completed the g when the lead broke again.

'It's a fake,' said Jemma, 'isn't it?'

'But I've got papers!' cried Sebastian.

'I don't care if you've got a telephone directory's worth,' said Dave. 'Off you go, Sebastian, and take that book with you. And since you tried to put one over on me, you needn't come back.'

'I assure you that this book is completely genuine,' said Sebastian, shooting Jemma an injured look. 'I don't see what a pencil has got to do with it.'

'Don't make me count to ten, Sebastian,' said Dave.

Sebastian strode off as if he had been insulted.

'That's saved me a lot of time and trouble, not to mention money,' said Dave. 'That charlatan's called in periodically for as long as I can remember, peddling various books of dubious authenticity, but I've never been able to pin him down until now.' He grinned. 'I'll take some money off your bill.'

Yes, a very satisfying day, thought Jemma, as she steered Gertrude through the quiet streets. She had taken the camper van to a quiet car park on the edge of a wood for lunch, and eaten her food surrounded by birdsong and the gentle whisper of leaves. When she finished, she decided to take a few minutes to peruse one of her new books, and found herself still reading an hour later. But when had she last taken a long lunch?

A visit to Elinor Dashwood, including of course the purchase of a few new books which Elinor had selected as just right for The Friendly Bookshop, finished the day off nicely. *I've bought new stock for the shop, unmasked a fraud, and given Gertrude a run out.* She glanced at the fuel gauge. *And I appear not to have used any petrol at all.*

When she pulled up at The Friendly Bookshop a few minutes later, Maddy came to help with the boxes. 'Gosh,' she said, when she looked in the back of Gertrude. 'That ought to keep us going.'

'We said that last time,' said Jemma, smiling. 'But yes, hopefully. Let's get them inside, then I can drop Gertrude home.'

Ten minutes later the shop was full of boxes, and Jemma drove the short distance to Burns Books. She was relieved to see that Luke was still behind the counter, though it was a quarter past five. 'Expecting someone?' she asked as she walked in, swinging Gertrude's keys on her finger.

'We are, actually,' said Luke. 'They've hired for the barista job.'

'We have,' said Raphael, coming through from the back

49

room with Giulia and Carl. 'Giulia has telephoned the successful candidate, who is popping back to sign the paperwork.'

'That was quick,' said Jemma.

'It was an easy decision,' said Carl, and Jemma felt just a little downcast that they had managed so well without her.

'I got back at the right time, then,' she said, holding out the keys to Raphael. 'I've unloaded Gertrude, and she's all yours.'

'Jolly good,' said Raphael. 'Ah, here she is.' He waved at the front door.

The shop bell rang and Jemma turned, ready to welcome the new employee. The pleasant words she had meant to utter froze on her tongue as she looked with dismay at the young, dark-haired, stylish woman before her.

'Hello, Jemma,' said Em.

Chapter 7

Jemma regarded Em for a long time, considering what to say. Em flinched under her gaze.

'I'm surprised to see you here,' said Jemma.

'Oh, so you know each other!' said Raphael. 'Excellent. I had no idea.'

'Yes, we used to know each other very well,' said Jemma, still glaring. 'Then we lost touch. Didn't we, Em?'

'Um, yes, when I moved to Scotland,' said Em, 'but it didn't work out.'

'I gathered,' said Jemma. 'So you're back.' Out of the corner of her eye, she saw Carl move. She glanced at him; he looked both hurt and angry. 'Raphael, I need a word.'

'What, now?' said Raphael. 'I thought we could get the paperwork done, then all go for a drink together.'

'I have to talk to you first,' said Jemma. 'It's urgent.'

'I deal with the paperwork, Raphael,' said Giulia

firmly. 'You talk to Jemma. Then we see.' She patted him on the arm. 'Come, Em, we go downstairs.'

Raphael waited until the great oak door downstairs had closed. 'I take it she isn't a friend,' he said, eyebrows raised.

'She was,' said Jemma. 'She was my best friend.' She stared at Raphael. 'You have no idea, do you?'

'That's true most of the time, frankly,' said Raphael. 'About what in particular?'

'Remember Damon Foskett?' asked Jemma, and had the satisfaction of watching Raphael's expression change. However, instead of the rage she had been expecting, his face showed mild amusement.

'The estate agent we sent for a little swim? Definitely.' His eyebrows drew together. 'What does Em have to do with him?'

'She's his girlfriend,' Jemma said, in an offhand manner. 'She tried to stop me taking the job here, and when I did, she tried to get me to leave. She knew exactly what he was up to. In fact, I reckon she helped him with the anonymous letters.'

'Are you sure?' asked Carl. 'She's really nice. And she said she was single.'

'She might be single now,' said Jemma, 'but she certainly wasn't then. And *then* was less than six months ago. I doubt she's changed so much.'

'Maybe she wasn't involved,' said Carl. 'You said she was what's-his-face's girlfriend. Maybe she knew something and she wanted to protect you.'

'I can see she's made a good impression on you,'

Jemma shot back.

'Don't be like that,' said Carl. 'She seems very capable, and she made the best cappuccino of all the candidates. We rang the owner of the café she worked at in Scotland, and he gave her a glowing reference.'

'That was probably a mate putting on a Scottish accent,' said Jemma. 'I'd follow that up with an email if I were you.'

'Whatever she's done,' said Raphael, 'she regrets it. She admitted at the interview that she'd taken a few wrong turns and she wants a fresh start.'

'I bet she does,' scoffed Jemma.

Raphael gave her a reproachful look. 'At any rate, she impressed all three of us – no, all four of us. Folio met the candidates too, and they got on very well. However you may rate our abilities to recruit a new team member, you can't deny that Folio is a good judge of character.'

'Remember when Luke first came into the shop and Folio scratched him?' asked Jemma, trying not to sound too triumphant.

'That was different,' said Luke, from behind the counter. Jemma jumped, having forgotten he was there. 'Folio didn't understand.'

'So he isn't infallible.' Jemma sighed. 'I can't believe I've told you this and you still want to employ her!'

'Maybe you should give her another chance,' said Raphael.

'She doesn't deserve one.'

'Come out for a drink, why don't you,' said Carl. 'Apart from anything else, we haven't done anything social as a team since the first night of the play.'

'Sorry, I've got new stock to deal with,' said Jemma. 'And then I might wash my hair.'

Carl glared at her. 'If I'm ever accused of a crime, I hope you won't be on the jury.' It was Jemma's turn to shoot him a hurt look. 'I'll go downstairs and see if anyone would like a drink,' he said, and loped off without a backward glance.

Jemma looked from Luke to Raphael and back, waiting for one of them to admit she had a point. Both shuffled their feet and remained silent.

'Fine,' she said, and slammed Gertrude's keys down on the counter. 'If you've got any sense, you'll ask her about Damon at the pub. Oh, and the anonymous letters. If you don't, and the shop's under threat by Christmas, don't blame me. If you want me, I'll be unpacking books.' She flung the shop door open with a mighty tinkle of the bell, and stomped out. *Fools!* she thought, as she power-walked to The Friendly Bookshop.

She found Maddy about to open a box of books. 'Are you all right?' Maddy asked, when she came through the door.

'No,' Jemma replied, 'I'm not. Don't ask me, Maddy, I'm too angry to talk about it. I'll see you tomorrow.'

Maddy gazed at her for a few seconds, then silently got her things and left.

Jemma locked the door behind her, then went and made herself a strong cup of tea. *That's the last time I let them interview without me*, she thought. *I don't care if she makes the best hot chocolate in London, I wouldn't touch*

Em with a barge pole. Once they've spent time with her, they'll agree with me. The snake!

One of the boxes she had brought back lay empty beside the counter, and the computer was on. When the screensaver disappeared, Jemma saw the database was open, with a message saying *New entry accepted.* From the lack of a pile of books, Maddy must have shelved the whole box. 'Thank you, Maddy,' she whispered. At least she could rely on someone. She sighed, and bent to open another box of books.

She had hoped the act of unpacking, recording and shelving her new acquisitions would be calming. Mostly it was, as she lifted out a book and remembered how pleased she had felt on coming across it, or when she looked at the shelves and saw the perfect place for it. But every so often, disturbing questions floated to the top of her mind and bobbed there, unwilling to go away. *Why won't they listen to me? Don't they trust me? They've only just met her; why are they listening to her and not me?* And perhaps worst of all: *Em's so good at everything. What if she decides she wants my job?* Jemma flicked her hair out of her eyes, picked up a stack of books, and marched off to the stockroom.

She was halfway through her task when her mobile rang. *Good*, she thought, wiping her hands on her jeans and fetching the phone from the counter. *Hopefully they've confronted her with it, and she's admitted everything.*

The display said *Em*.

Jemma stared at it for two more rings, then huffed and punched the *Accept* button. 'Yes?' she barked.

'I'm sorry,' said Em. 'I didn't realise when I applied that it was your shop.'

'I suppose that's something,' said Jemma. 'I didn't think even you would have the nerve to go after a job at the shop you tried to destroy.'

'That wasn't me!' cried Em. 'That was Damon. And when I figured out it was the shop you worked at, it was too late.'

'Rubbish,' said Jemma. 'You could have come clean to me at any time, and you didn't. You backed him.'

'I loved him,' said Em. 'I bet you'd have done the same.'

'I wouldn't fall in love with someone who could do such a thing,' said Jemma.

'It isn't as easy as that,' said Em, in a small voice.

'Huh,' said Jemma. 'I bet you never thought about what you were doing to the bookshop. Or me.' She paused. 'So, have they found out what you're really like and sacked you yet?'

Silence. 'We went to the pub for a drink,' said Em. 'But before we left, Raphael took me aside—'

'Mr Burns to you,' snapped Jemma.

'He told me to call him Raphael,' said Em quietly. 'He said you'd made your concerns known, and we'd see how things went.'

I don't believe this, thought Jemma. *This is some sort of nightmare, like one of those fly-on-the-wall TV shows. When Recruitment Goes Wrong: 5.*

'I'm coming in tomorrow to shadow Carl,' said Em, 'and I'm helping with the refreshments at the evening meeting. I thought I should mention it in case you'd rather not see me yet.'

'I'd rather not see you at all,' said Jemma. 'I wish you were still in Scotland, or preferably further away. In fact, Antarctica's still a bit close for my liking.'

A sniffle on the other end of the line. 'I didn't think this would be easy,' said Em, 'but I need this job. Please let me try, Jemma, and maybe in time you'll be able to trust me again.'

'I wouldn't trust you as far as I could throw you,' said Jemma, and ended the call. A grim smile spread across her face. *She may be able to charm the rest of them, but there's no way she's getting round me.* She made herself a fresh drink, and tackled the next box.

Maybe they're still in the pub, she thought, when she had three boxes left to deal with. She reached for her mobile and texted Carl: *Are you lot still drinking? I might be able to get there in half an hour x.* She felt tired and grimy, and would really prefer a hot bath, a glass of wine, and a bowl of pasta to the pub. But if Em could go to the bookshop social, she was darned if she'd be left out.

She unpacked the next box and updated the database, checking her phone every so often for a reply. Nothing. Then she checked to see if the message had sent. Apparently, it had. *His phone's probably in his pocket. I'll finish these boxes, then I'll ring.*

One box later her willpower gave way and she dialled his number. It rang four times. *Not straight to voicemail. Good.* But the seventh ring stopped part way through. 'Hello, this is Carl's voicemail—'

Jemma ended the call abruptly and stared at her phone. Carl's mobile never went through to voicemail in the middle of the ring. *He refused the call. Maybe she's still there, or—* She brushed her hair out of her eyes and blinked. *Or he's still angry with me.*

Fine. Just fine. I'm not the one who's in the wrong here, and they'll find that out soon enough. She went to open the next box, then had a better idea and picked up the phone again. 'Hello? I'd like to order a pizza to be delivered. Yes, it is me. Yes, the usual. Fifteen minutes? Great. Bye.' She rubbed her eyes; it was amazing how dust got into everything.

Jemma attacked the final box with gusto. *Once this is done I can eat pizza, have a glass of wine, maybe another in the bath, then fall into bed. They may be having a good time now, but they'll regret it later.* And with that satisfying thought, she set another pile of books on the counter.

Chapter 8

Jemma took a deep breath and pushed open the door of Burns Books.

Raphael looked up from his newspaper. 'Morning, Jemma.'

'Good morning,' said Jemma. She took off her jacket and hung it up. 'I'll work on the upstairs till today, if that's OK.'

'I had a feeling you'd say that,' said Raphael. 'If you want to go downstairs and get a coffee, Em isn't due in until ten.'

'I see,' said Jemma. 'Thanks.'

'Please give her a chance,' said Raphael.

'I'll be polite,' said Jemma. 'It's up to her to make me change my mind, not the other way round.' She took her purse from her bag and went downstairs.

Carl was loading Danish pastries and other treats into

the display cabinet. As Jemma approached, she realised he was watching her through the glass. 'Hi,' she said. 'Could I have a cappuccino, please?'

'Sure,' said Carl, without his usual smile. He turned to the coffee machine and began the ritual.

'It's the meeting tonight, isn't it?' said Jemma, to break the silence. 'Will you stay?'

'Yes,' said Carl. 'I'll be showing Em the ropes.' A hiss from the coffee machine made Jemma jump, but he carried on preparing her drink in silence.

'Here you go,' he said, putting it down.

Jemma opened her purse.

'Don't be silly.' Carl picked up a cloth and became very busy wiping the coffee machine.

I hate it when you're like this, thought Jemma. She wanted to say something to snap him out of it, but she suspected he was looking for *I'm sorry* or *You were right*, and she wasn't prepared to say either. So she took her cappuccino and went upstairs.

She found Raphael in the shop doorway, glancing this way and that. 'Are you scouting for customers?' she asked.

'Cats,' replied Raphael. 'Folio's gone off again. He had his breakfast then demanded to be let out, and I haven't seen him since.' He frowned. 'I hope he doesn't get into another fight.'

'He'll be fine,' said Jemma. 'Why don't you find a nice novel to distract you? Worrying won't bring him back any faster.'

'You're probably right,' said Raphael. 'It's unlike him to wander, though. He's always been a shop cat.' He glanced at Jemma. 'There's something I wanted to ask you.'

Jemma braced herself for an interrogation about her former friendship with Em.

'Have you set a date for the management strategies committee meeting? I had a message from Drusilla yesterday.'

Jemma took the lid off her cappuccino and sipped it, to gain time. 'The novel group meeting is tomorrow,' she said, reasonably. 'I thought it best to attend that first and get a feel for how these groups work. Then I can set a date and send out the agenda next week.'

'Mmm,' said Raphael. 'I hoped to get back to Drusilla today.'

'Another factor,' said Jemma, clutching at straws, 'is that we don't know what will happen at this evening's meeting.'

'Oh, very well,' said Raphael. 'I'll let Drusilla know you have it in hand.' The shop bell jingled. 'Hello, Em, you're early.'

'Hello, Raphael,' said Em, smiling at him. 'Hello, Jemma.' The smile was still there, but had become polite rather than warm.

'Hello,' said Jemma. 'I'll let you two get on.' She walked over to a shelf in the far corner and stood there, studying the books. The travel section was looking sparse. She went to the stockroom, got a box, and carried it through to the counter. However, when she opened it she was greeted not with the Rough Guides and Lonely Planet books she had been expecting, but books with cats on the cover. The top two were *Caring For Your Cat* and *Feline Great: Your Cat's Emotional Wellbeing*.

Jemma opened her mouth to say something to Raphael, then stopped. No way was she letting Em into any of the shop's secrets. Instead, she closed the box and waited until Raphael and Em had gone downstairs before replacing the box in the stockroom and fetching another. But that was no better.

She walked across to the front door and pulled it open. *Where's Folio?* She gazed up and down the street just as Raphael had, expecting nothing. But trotting towards her, tail a bobbing question mark, was the cat himself. He meowed in greeting as he slipped into the shop.

'Honestly, Folio,' said Jemma. 'Where have you been this time?' He jumped onto the counter and she stroked him. 'We need our bookshop cat.'

Folio purred and rubbed his chin against the corner of the book box. When Jemma opened it, she found the travel guides she wanted.

Her morning at Burns Books was quiet and pleasant. Normally she would have finished it by eating lunch in the café, assuming there was room. Today, though, she had a sandwich waiting for her in her flat. She waited for a lull, then went down and waved to Raphael from the doorway. 'I'm off now,' she called. 'I'll send Luke back.'

Raphael finished serving his customer, then came over. 'Thanks, Jemma. Everything all right up there?'

'Folio's returned,' said Jemma. 'Have you been finding cat books in the stockroom?'

Raphael considered. 'I don't think so. I'd have

remembered.'

'Just me, then,' said Jemma. 'It's stopped now, anyway. See you at the meeting.'

When she returned to The Friendly Bookshop, Maddy and Luke fell silent, their faces blank. 'Is everything OK?' she asked.

'Everything's fine,' said Luke. 'I'll be off.' He looked out of the window. 'Sunshine,' he muttered. He put on his sunglasses and beanie hat. 'See you later, Jemma.'

'Yes, see you later,' said Jemma. She watched him go, then turned to Maddy. 'Is there anything I ought to know about?'

'Oh no,' said Maddy. 'Nothing to worry about. It's been quite a dull morning.' She bit her lip. 'Oh, a cat came in,' she said casually.

'A cat?' asked Jemma. 'Not Folio? He went for another wander this morning.'

'No,' said Maddy, and Jemma saw she was struggling not to smile. 'A black cat, with green eyes and no collar. She must have slipped in with a customer. I didn't notice a thing until I went into the back and nearly tripped over her.'

'Hopefully that's lucky,' said Jemma. She frowned. 'How do you know the cat's female?'

'She looks like a female cat,' said Maddy, nodding wisely. 'Would you mind if I took an early lunch today?'

'Go for it,' said Jemma. 'I'll just nip upstairs and get mine.'

Probably a coincidence, she thought as she climbed the stairs. *The cat books appeared because Folio went missing again*. She grabbed her tuna sandwich from the fridge, took a banana and apple from the fruit bowl, and pulled the door closed behind her.

'I'll be off, then,' said Maddy as soon as she returned. She was already waiting by the door.

Is everyone avoiding me today? Even Burns Books had been quiet. But it had been nice to get on with her admin rather than dash around keeping the customers happy and the shelves filled. *You'll wish for quiet days in the week before Christmas*, she told herself. Then she went to make a cup of tea and found a small bowl on the floor, half filled with water, and a side plate with a few flakes of salmon left on it. Jemma sighed, and cleared them away.

***

That evening, Jemma arrived at Burns Books at ten to seven. 'You'll be lucky to get a seat,' said Luke, who was on the door. 'It's heaving.' And indeed, when she went downstairs the café area was already full. She recognised the shopkeepers from the parade – Jim, Nafisa, Dave, Giulia, and Nathan the estate agent, whom she only knew because she'd seen him often in Rolando's, his name badge still on. However, she also saw several faces she didn't recognise and some she wouldn't have expected to see, like the man from the hardware shop, and Eileen who ran the charity shop a few doors down.

'Jemma!' Raphael was sitting at a table with Maddy and Carl. Giulia wasn't with him, but sitting at a table with her own staff.

Mr Tennant was roaming around with his clipboard, having a word here and there. 'We'll begin at seven on the dot,' he said. He consulted his watch. 'Four minutes and . . . twenty seconds to go.'

The room was filled with chatter, and Jemma noticed copies of the flyer Raphael had received being passed around. She walked over and took the seat he had saved for her. 'It's a good turnout, isn't it?'

'It is,' he replied. 'I wonder what everyone wants.'

'Well,' Jemma said, as Luke entered the room, 'I guess we'll find out soon.'

'I would like to call this meeting to order,' said Mr Tennant, in a carrying voice he was clearly comfortable with using. 'This is an extraordinary meeting of the Westminster Retailers' Association, Charing Cross Branch. The purpose of this meeting is to discuss the flyer which some of our members have received, with an offer to purchase their premises at what seems a very fair price.'

'Yes, but at what cost?' asked Giulia. 'Rolando's is not just a building.'

Mr Tennant gave her a tolerant look. 'Before we start expressing opinions,' he said, 'we should take care of the housekeeping,' and proceeded to go through safety precautions, emergency exits, toilets, and amenities. 'I think that's everything,' he said, five minutes later. 'As I understand it, the flyer, which all of you have now seen, has been received by the proprietors of six shops on Charing Cross Road which form a small parade.'

'That is my understanding too,' said a small, desiccated man sitting at a table on his own. 'As the owner of one of those premises, namely the unit housing Ransome's estate agency, I think the offer a good one, and I have every intention of taking it up.' Nathan and the rest of the agency staff appeared rather dismayed at the thought that they themselves might be property hunting.

'Me too,' said Jim. 'You can open an antique shop anywhere. I don't mind renting somewhere and investing a nice chunk of cash.'

'We have no intention of going anywhere,' said Raphael.

'Neither do we,' Giulia echoed, and her staff rumbled a confirmation.

'I don't particularly want to move,' said Dave from Snacking Cross Road, 'but I don't own the shop. So we'll see.'

'Do you know who is behind this?' asked Eileen. 'It would help if we knew whether some shops might be sold, or whether the intention would be to pull down the parade and build something else.'

Mr Tennant looked regretful. 'Unfortunately, at this moment in time, we are not aware of this piece of information.'

A dry cough came from the small man. 'I phoned the number on the flyer, which is how I obtained my quote,' he said. 'The person I spoke to said they were an employee of DZD Holdings.' He gave Mr Tennant a withering glance. 'A few minutes with a smartphone would tell you that DZD Holdings have various interests in construction, so we can safely assume they are not planning to keep the parade as it is.' He smiled a wintry smile. 'Let's face it, it's an eyesore, and I don't think anyone would be too sorry to bid it farewell.'

'I had a chap in my shop the other day,' said Colin the barber. 'A construction worker, and he said there were plans to build a new cinema.'

'A friend of mine works in the planning department at the council,' said the man from the hardware store, 'and he said they've just granted permission for a new supermarket.' Nafisa scowled at him.

'What they want to put there doesn't matter,' said Raphael. 'Presumably all of us must agree to sell, or else there is no deal.'

A gluey chuckle came from the man in the corner. 'Unless they play the compulsory purchase card, and then you'll have no choice.' His pale eyes gleamed like a five-pence piece in the gutter, and the floor trembled as if an underground train were passing underneath. 'They'll play nice for the moment, but when those gloves come off, old chap, you'll feel it.'

Chapter 9

'Do you think it's important that bookshops stay open?' asked Maddy, fixing the customer with a beady eye.

The customer took a step back. 'Er, yes, of course I do. I mean, I'm in a bookshop.' She peered at Maddy. 'Are you thinking of changing the opening hours?'

'Not this bookshop,' said Maddy, impatiently. 'Our sister bookshop, Burns Books, is under threat. We've got a petition you can sign, and we are asking people to write to the council too.'

'Um, I'm in rather a hurry today,' said the customer. 'Maybe the next time I'm in.' She grabbed her bag of books, clutching it to her chest as if Maddy might wrest it from her, and fled.

'She could at least have signed the petition,' said Maddy. 'Or taken a sticker.'

'Maddy, at this rate we'll be closing, not Burns Books,'

said Jemma. 'I understand you're passionate about it, but we can't afford to drive customers away. Especially not before Christmas.'

'Someone's got to do something,' said Maddy, counting the signatures on the clipboard once more. 'Hopefully Luke is doing better.'

'I'm sure he's doing fine,' soothed Jemma. 'Anyway, we don't want to get the bookshop worked up, do we?'

'S'pose,' muttered Maddy.

Yesterday's meeting, in the end, had been short. Raphael had suggested a refreshment break immediately after the small man had dropped his bombshell about compulsory purchase, hoping to distract the shop, and to a degree it had worked. Em, unprepared for a sudden deluge of people all wanting hot drinks at the same time, had looked completely out of her depth. Carl had had to rush to the rescue, dealing with the more complicated orders while Em dispensed cups of tea, Americanos, and caffè lattes.

While that had given Jemma some satisfaction, it was a lone bright spot in an otherwise grim evening. She had patrolled the room listening to conversations; people's responses to the news ranged from enthusiasm through resignation to frank opposition. Once everybody reconvened, it was clear there was no hope of either resolution or compromise. Mr Tennant had been forced to call the meeting to order, said rather weakly that he would see what he could find out, and promised to send the minutes as soon as they were ready.

When everyone had dispersed, which took some time since most were not ready to leave their comfortable chairs or finish their drinks, Jemma locked the door behind the last attendee and went back downstairs. Giulia was clearing tables, her mouth in a firm line. Maddy and Luke were sitting close together and whispering conspiratorially, with occasional glances at the others, and Raphael was sitting slightly apart, slowly shaking his head.

'A campaign, that's what we need,' Luke said decisively. 'Banners and posters.'

'But you heard what that guy said,' Jemma replied. 'If whoever wants the parade can do a compulsory purchase, none of that would help.'

'Maybe I could do something,' said a quiet voice from the café counter. Em stood there, a tea towel over her shoulder.

'Like what, exactly?' asked Jemma, doing her best not to sound sarcastic.

'I know Nathan and a couple of the other staff at Ransome's, through Damon,' said Em. 'They know much more about this sort of thing than we do, and they have contacts at the council. It's a long shot, but—'

'But it might just work!' said Carl. 'Genius, Em.' He saw Jemma's expression and the grin vanished from his face. 'I mean, it's definitely something to work on.'

'We can give it a try,' said Raphael. 'Though I'm not optimistic.' He ran his hand along the edge of the café table as if soothing it. 'I'm glad the shop didn't react too badly.'

'Me too,' said Jemma. She remembered the time when the shop had plunged itself into darkness and cut off its own power, as well as that of the whole parade, and shivered.

'So that means I can go ahead?' said Em, looking straight at her.

Jemma met her gaze, considering how to phrase her reply. It wasn't a bad idea, certainly – in fact, she was cross she hadn't thought of it. She shrugged. 'You might as well. I don't suppose it can hurt.'

'I'll do my best,' said Em, quietly, and Jemma fought the urge to make gagging noises and mime sticking a finger down her throat. *Honestly, talk about milking it.*

Luke and Maddy left, whispering fiercely to each other, and the others weren't long in making moves to depart. 'Anyone fancy a drink?' said Carl, looking around the group.

'Wouldn't mind,' said Em. She shot a quick glance at Jemma, but said nothing.

Carl raised his eyebrows. 'Jemma, want to come?'

At least he asked me. But there was no way she was ready for a convivial evening in the pub with Em. Too much had happened between them. 'Sorry, got some reading to do,' she said. 'Maybe another time. Bye, everyone.' Ignoring Carl's exasperated glance, she slung her jacket over her shoulder and left, hoping Raphael and Giulia would join Carl and Em for a drink. *Still don't trust you, Em.* Anyway, she did have reading to do. The novel discussion group was tomorrow morning, and she was still only halfway through *The History Of The Novel.* She got three-quarters of the way through the book before deciding her brain wasn't capable of holding any more, and switched to her current Marian Keyes instead. *That's more*

71

like it.

***

Jemma checked the clock: five to ten. *Nearly time.* She swallowed. 'Maddy, I have to dial into a meeting, and it's probably best to do it upstairs. Will you be all right here on your own?'

'Oh yes,' said Maddy, straightening the clipboard that held the petition, and watching the next customer enter as an eagle might watch a mouse.

'Please don't scare them off, Maddy,' Jemma murmured, and went upstairs.

At least I'm not chairing this, she thought, as she opened her email and clicked the link that Raphael had sent her. *I don't even have to talk.*

She gazed at the screen, expecting to find herself in a waiting room, but the meeting window opened immediately and eleven other faces gazed at her. 'Um, hello,' she said. 'Am I late?'

'No, not at all,' said an earnest woman with an ash-blonde bob. 'We were discussing what books people are buying and borrowing in the run-up to Christmas. Novels, obviously.'

'Oh, I see,' said Jemma, taken aback. 'I suppose most people who buy now are getting presents, rather than books for themselves.'

The woman laughed. 'Quite possibly. Of course, so much of it is driven by what the newspapers recommend. Anyway.' She smiled. 'My name is Alice, and I am the acting chairperson of this group since Brian's departure. You must be Jemma.' She paused. 'Did you read the

72

minutes of the last meeting?'

'Oh yes,' Jemma assured her. 'They were good. Very succinct.' That was the only thing she remembered about them, as she had no knowledge of at least half the topics which the minutes said the group had discussed.

Alice bit her lip. 'I'm afraid I have a confession, Jemma. That was the group's first meeting without Brian, and while he had sent out the agenda before his, um, departure, I'm afraid none of us had a clue what he was on about. We generally didn't, you see. So we had a nice chat over coffee and made up the minutes.' A stricken expression crossed her face. 'So if you want a discussion of the emerging tropes in the twenty-first-century literary novel, I'm afraid you'll be disappointed.'

'Oh,' said Jemma, looking serious. 'Oh dear.'

Eleven worried faces gazed back at her.

'In that case,' she said, with a grin, 'I'm very relieved indeed. I've been dreading this meeting, and worrying that you would be horrible about the books I love reading. Wait a minute.' She dived into her bag and held up her current book. 'What are you all reading at the moment?' And a delighted buzz filled the screen.

***

'I take it you enjoyed yourself,' Maddy said rather sourly when Jemma bounded downstairs two hours later. 'I could hear you giggling up there from the counter.'

'We were having a literary discussion,' said Jemma. Then she grinned. 'Actually, we were talking books. It was great. We're thinking of changing the name of the group.'

'Good for you,' said Maddy, rolling her eyes. 'May I go

for lunch? I've been running between here and the stockroom all morning.'

Jemma felt a pang of guilt. 'Of course you can, Maddy.'

'I'll go and see how Luke is getting on,' said Maddy. She went into the back room, retrieved a tub of salad from the fridge, and strolled off.

When she had gone, Jemma hugged herself with glee and sheer relief. She hadn't realised how much the prospect of the meeting had weighed her down. Although now, of course, there was the Management Strategies group to sort out. *Next week,* she thought. *I'm not letting it cast a cloud over my weekend—*

Eeep.

Jemma frowned. The noise sounded as if it had come from the back room. It resembled nothing so much as a squeaky floorboard. *But no one else is here.* She held her breath, and listened.

Eeep.

Maybe it's mice, thought Jemma. She hoped so. Mice, while troublesome, would be considerably less troubling than an intruder sneaking in when their backs were turned. *Maddy wouldn't have been so distracted as to let someone come in and hide...* Then she remembered Maddy had spent time in the stockroom. *Even so...*

Just in case it wasn't mice, she selected a heavy but not especially valuable hardback from the nearest shelf and advanced stealthily towards the back of the shop.

Eeep.

You had better be a mouse, thought Jemma. Thoroughly riled, she strode through to the back room, the book raised in her right hand. What she saw made her stop, and lower it.

Sitting in the middle of the floor, very upright, round green eyes fixed on Jemma, was a large black cat. She swished her tail once, then curled it around her paws, which were placed neatly together. Then she opened her pink mouth, and squeaked again.

Chapter 10

Still keeping her eyes on the cat, Jemma put the book on the worktop. She reached down to her jeans pocket and felt the familiar shape of her mobile phone. *Good.* Still watching the cat, she dialled the number of Burns Books.

Raphael answered, as she had hoped he would. 'Good morning – I mean good afternoon, Burns Books.'

'Hi, Raphael,' said Jemma. 'We've got a situation.'

A pause. 'What sort of situation?'

'A black, furry situation.' The cat confirmed this by squeaking.

Raphael was silent for a moment. 'Does it have a tail?'

'It does.'

'Pointy ears? Whiskers?'

Jemma studied the cat. 'Affirmative.'

'Do you think it's a cat?'

Jemma laughed. 'Of course it's a cat, what else would it

be?'

'If you'd seen what I've seen…' Raphael said darkly. 'Is it friendly?'

Jemma considered. 'It's squeaking at me.'

'So not unfriendly, at the very least.' Jemma heard the scuffle of a hand over the receiver for a few moments, then Raphael came back on the line. 'I'll be there in a few minutes.'

'Thank you—' Jemma began, but he had already rung off. She put the phone in her pocket and looked at the cat, who swished her tail then tucked it round her feet again. 'What am I going to do with you?'

The cat yawned, showing pointy white fangs.

'OK, I'm not coming near you.' Jemma took a step back and Raphael's words echoed in her head: If you'd seen what I've seen… *Of course it's a cat,* she told herself. *Just because I work in a bookshop with a tendency to magic, that doesn't mean everything that comes in is a were-cat, or a vampire cat, or—*

Those fangs, though. Jemma inched towards the worktop, checked the water level in the kettle, and flicked it on. Whatever she was facing, she would be able to manage it better with a cup of tea.

The shop bell rang. 'Hello?' called Raphael. 'Anyone home?'

'I'm in the back.'

Raphael appeared in the doorway, a cat carrier in his hand, closely followed by Folio.

Jemma raised her eyebrows. 'Was it a good idea to bring Folio?'

Raphael shrugged. 'It wasn't up to me.'

Folio trotted forward and touched noses with the black cat, who looked startled. She stood up and stretched – *How long she is*, thought Jemma – and the pair of them circled each other, nose to tail.

'They won't fight, will they?' asked Jemma. A thought struck her. 'Do you think this is how Folio hurt his ear?'

'I wouldn't be surprised,' replied Raphael. 'In which case, this possibly isn't your average cat.'

Having completed a few circuits, the black cat walked into the main shop and investigated the shelves, sniffing at a book here and there, and occasionally sneezing. Jemma made a mental note to revisit her dusting schedule. Folio followed and leapt onto the counter, watching.

'What do I do?' asked Jemma.

Raphael held up the cat carrier. 'The first thing to do is get her into this, take her to the vet or an animal shelter, and find out if she's microchipped. Then we'll know if she has an owner. Maybe the vet could put up a poster, or you could post something on social media.'

The black cat trotted to the wastepaper basket, put her front paws on the rim, and stuck her head inside. She emerged with a small ball of paper held carefully in her mouth, which she dropped on the floor and began to bat between her paws.

'She's playing football!' said Jemma, leaning forward.

A forceful swipe sent the paper ball underneath the bookshelf. After a couple of attempts to reach under, the black cat turned to them and squeaked.

'Oh, she's only young,' said Raphael. 'She hasn't got a

proper meow yet.'

'I suppose we ought to take her to the vet,' said Jemma, 'and see if she has an owner.' She went over to the bookcase, retrieved the ball, and threw it underarm. Folio launched himself into the air, a ginger blur, and the two cats raced after it.

The door opened and Maddy stopped dead as two furry streaks shot across her path. 'Ooh!' she cried. 'You came back!'

Jemma folded her arms. 'So this is the cat who visited before?'

'Might be,' said Maddy. 'She's moving a bit too fast to tell.'

'Is this the reason for the tins of salmon and pouches of cat food in the back-room cupboard?' asked Jemma.

'I like salmon,' said Maddy. 'And it's always good to be prepared. Luna likes salmon too.' She bent down. 'Don't you?'

The black cat dropped her paper ball and squeaked, then strolled over to Maddy with panther-like grace and allowed her to stroke her head.

'Luna?' asked Jemma. 'I'm not sure we should start naming cats who aren't ours.'

'Yet,' said Maddy, scratching behind Luna's ears.

***

Jemma phoned Raphael from outside the vet's surgery. 'No, there's no microchip, and as far as they know, no one is missing a black cat. They said she's healthy and maybe a year old.'

Luna squeaked from inside the carrier. Jemma had been

79

extremely surprised when she had walked into it without a fuss, but Maddy said that showed what an excellent cat she was. 'Aren't you, Luna?' She poked a finger through the wire door and Luna rubbed her chin against it.

'So what will you do?' asked Raphael. 'I suppose you could take her to a shelter.'

'She isn't going to a shelter,' said Jemma. 'We've got cat food at the bookshop, and we can put a blanket in a box for now, and if she likes paper balls, we've got plenty of those. All we need is a litter tray.'

'So you're set up, then,' said Raphael.

'Yes, we are,' said Jemma, as she opened the door of The Friendly Bookshop. The first thing she saw was Maddy's questioning face. *No owner*, she mouthed, and Maddy beamed. 'I'll sort that out, and then we'll come over for Carl's leaving drinks.' She had only remembered that today was his official last day when she was sitting in the vet's waiting room, at a loose end for what felt like the first time that day. 'Do you need me to bring anything?'

'No, we're all sorted,' said Raphael. 'Em has been busy.'

I bet she has, thought Jemma, but said nothing. 'I'll see you soon, then,' she said, and ended the call.

A squeak from the cat carrier indicated that Luna was more than ready to come out. Jemma put down the carrier and unlatched the door, and Luna strolled out as if stepping from a sports car.

'Oh, isn't she elegant?' said a customer. 'Is she the bookshop cat?'

Luna sashayed towards the customer and looked up at

her, purring.

'She seems to think so,' said Jemma.

***

In an almost unprecedented move, Jemma closed The Friendly Bookshop at four thirty. 'It isn't as if one of our staff leaves every day,' she said. 'Although Carl isn't leaving, exactly—'

'Well, he is,' said Maddy, as they walked down the road together. 'He said he might be available for an occasional shift, but really—'

'Don't make it worse,' said Jemma.

When they arrived, they found the party in full swing. The bookshop regulars had been invited, and the lower floor of the bookshop was full of people. Raphael had even moved some bookshelves against the wall to create a makeshift dance floor, and customers of all shapes and sizes were exhibiting a surprising variety of moves. Giulia was behind the café counter, serving hot drinks and snacks, while Em was circulating with a tray of drinks. Carl himself, meanwhile, had been backed into a corner by the two Golden Age crime ladies, who were both talking and gesticulating. He shot a *help me* look at Jemma, who giggled and went to rescue him.

'Thanks,' he said, under his breath. 'They were asking for my views on Agatha Christie dramatisations. I didn't think I'd get out alive.'

'Let's get a drink,' said Jemma.

'Did someone say drink?' Em had appeared from nowhere. 'Buck's Fizz, Bellini or Kir Royale?'

'Gosh,' said Jemma. 'Go on, I'll have a Kir Royale.'

81

She turned to Carl. 'Has Raphael told you about our new member of staff yet?'

Carl's face immediately assumed a guarded expression. 'Um, should we have this conversation later?'

Jemma raised her eyebrows. 'So he didn't mention the cat?'

'Oh, the cat! Yes, of course. I thought you meant—'

He thought I meant Em. 'No, I was talking about Luna.' Jemma glanced at the place where Em had been, but she had vanished. *How can I manage to put my foot in it without meaning to so many times?* She took a large sip of her drink. 'Shall we dance?'

They had finished their drinks, had a quick break for a sustaining sausage roll, and sampled another cocktail when Jemma heard banging on the door upstairs. 'Latecomers, I guess,' she bellowed into Carl's ear. 'I'd better let them in.' She gave him a quick kiss, then ran upstairs, stumbling slightly. *Maybe a soft drink next.*

There were two bulky shapes beyond the glass, but it was too dark to see much more. She unlocked the door and threw it open. Standing on the doorstep were two men she couldn't place, both wearing raincoats. One was tall and thin and carried a briefcase, the other short and broad, wearing a bowler hat. 'Welcome!' she cried. 'You're a bit late, but there's plenty of food left and we haven't started the speeches yet.'

The two men entered the shop, looking around them. 'I wasn't aware this was also a party venue,' said the taller one.

Jemma's eyes widened. 'Aren't you here for Carl's

leaving drinks? We do have a licence.'

'I'm sure you do,' said the short broad one. 'And no, we're not.' He took off his hat. 'Allow us to introduce ourselves. I am Mr Bunce, and my companion is Mr Tipping. We did phone ahead, but nobody answered.' A smile crept across his face. 'We are from the council, and we're here about a compulsory purchase order. Everyone is downstairs, I take it?' He sauntered through the shop as if he knew it intimately, followed by Mr Tipping, and Jemma was powerless to stop them.

Chapter 11

In Jemma's more carefree student days, she had watched a lot of films. She was aware of the classic scene where someone walks into a bar and all music and conversation stops as everyone eyes the newcomer. However, she had never seen it happen in real life before. Then again, she had the feeling Mr Bunce and Mr Tipping probably had that effect whenever they walked into a room.

Mr Bunce took off his hat and rested it on his chest, as if about to offer his condolences. 'I'm looking for Mr Raphael Burns.'

Raphael, who had been cutting a dash on the dance floor, straightened his bow tie guiltily and walked towards the two men. 'I am he.'

'Oh good. I am Mr Bunce, from the council, and we are here to inform you of the possibility of a compulsory purchase order on your property.'

The silence that followed was deeper than Jemma had believed silence could be.

Raphael drew himself up. 'And what exactly are you proposing to do with my property?'

Mr Bunce laughed. '*I'm* not proposing to do anything.' He addressed the crowd. 'Don't you find,' he said, conversationally, 'that central London is getting increasingly difficult to navigate?'

A rumble of agreement, and a few nods.

'Gridlocked traffic, crowded streets, tube trains so full you can't even get on them…' He glanced at his audience to judge the effect. 'What the council are proposing will make things much easier. An underground transport hub will connect multiple tube stations, allowing both commuters and residents to go about their day in peace.' He clicked his fingers twice. 'Mr Tipping, the artist's impressions, if you would.'

Mr Tipping opened his briefcase and extracted a roll of paper.

'No, thank you,' said Raphael. 'I don't want to see any artist's impressions of what the world would look like without this bookshop, and I wish to hear no more. This is a private gathering, now we are outside shop hours, and you are not invited.' Jemma hoped she was the only one who could detect a note of uncertainty beneath those confident words.

Mr Bunce shook his head sadly. 'Now, Mr Burns, that's not the right attitude. This will happen, like it or not.'

'Why haven't we heard anything about it?' asked Em. 'Why hasn't there been a public consultation?' She surveyed the crowd. 'Have any of you heard about this before?'

A general muttering and shaking of heads. For the first time ever, Jemma was glad that Em was there.

Mr Bunce favoured her with a jovial leer. 'Someone's been reading up, I see,' he said. 'You're quite right, my dear. Our visit today is the beginning of the public consultation. The clock, as you might put it, starts now.' He tapped his watch. 'Now, I'd love to tell you more about the built-in retail offerings, the proposed measures to improve the environment, and the carbon-neutral credentials of the proposed development, but unfortunately Mr Burns here won't let me. So I'll just have to tell you that information will be available at every public library in Westminster, as well as the council offices, from Monday.' He pulled a bundle of flyers from his raincoat pocket and placed them on the counter. 'I'll leave these here and be on my way.' He put his hat back on. 'Mr Tipping!' he barked.

Mr Tipping, whose hand was about to close on a glass of Buck's Fizz, jumped and slunk after Mr Bunce.

Mr Bunce had reached the great oak door when he paused. 'Oh yes,' he said. 'I almost forgot to mention the money.' He extracted a card case from his pocket, scribbled a number on the back of a card in pencil, walked across the room and held it out to Raphael. 'A generous offer, if I may say so.'

Raphael folded his arms. 'I don't care how much it is,' he said. 'I'm not selling.'

'You may not have a choice,' said Mr Bunce, grinning. 'But have it your own way.' He let go of the card, which fell to the floor.

As he walked to the door, the floor trembled and the lights flickered. Mr Bunce stopped and gazed around him. 'That isn't very good, is it?' he said, with a censorious expression. 'Maybe you should accept this offer before the place falls down.' The bang of the door behind him sounded like the closing of a tomb.

'Someone put the music back on,' said Raphael. 'I'm not letting that pair of bureaucrats spoil our evening.'

Luke shrugged and walked across to the tablet and Bluetooth speaker sitting on the shop counter. 'Money For Nothing' rang out for a few bars before Luke skipped the track.

'Roadblock'. *Skip.*

'Dirty Cash'. *Skip.*

'Bills Bills Bills'. The music ended.

People began to move towards the door, saying that it had been a lovely evening but they needed to get home to watch the news, help the children with homework, put dinner on... Some murmured 'Good luck' to Carl. Jemma noted that most of them took a flyer from the pile on the counter.

Felicity, who was holding hands with Jerome, let go briefly to pick up Mr Bunce's card. She handed it to Raphael. 'That's a lot of money,' she said, eyes wide. 'I'm sure you could buy another shop just as nice. Maybe even nicer.'

'That isn't the point,' said Raphael.

'I'm only saying,' said Felicity, and walked away with Jerome.

Within five minutes all the guests were on their way. Jemma heard snatches of the conversation as they passed her.

'If they did it well, it could be really good...'

'I'd miss this place, but he could move somewhere more modern.'

'The air is so dirty around here. Anything to improve that must be a good thing.'

Raphael sank into a chair and put his head in his hands. 'Listen to them,' he murmured. 'They've already made up their minds.'

Jemma sat down beside him. 'Never mind them,' she said. 'At least, not now. Can't you do something in your' – she glanced at Em – 'your other capacity? Or ask Armand Dupont to intervene?'

Raphael shook his head. 'I wish I could, but it would mean exposing the Guild. We can't allow that to happen.'

'There must be something we can do,' said Carl, sitting down on Raphael's other side.

'There is,' said Jemma. 'We're going to fight this.' Maddy and Luke were standing together, hand in hand, like two lost children. 'You were right, and I was wrong,' she said. 'We'll do everything we can. Get the other shopkeepers together, lobby the council, go to consultation meetings and raise objections, get signatures on the petition...'

'I can get the arts centre to spread the word,' said Carl.

'We will in Rolando's too,' said Giulia. She walked over to Raphael, put a hand on his shoulder, then lifted his chin gently. 'We get through this, mio caro.'

'Now we know more, I'll talk to the estate agents again,' said Em. 'And I'll track down the consultation documents. I bet there's a way we can stop it.'

Raphael raised a hand. 'All right, but not tonight. I've had enough, and I suspect the shop has too.' He looked around. 'Where's Folio?'

'He'll be somewhere,' soothed Jemma. 'He's probably upstairs, wondering why you haven't fed him.' She hoped Folio hadn't chosen this moment to wander off. 'Anyone want to go for a drink?' She eyed the few remaining cocktails. 'Or have one here?'

Everyone shook their heads, muttering about an early night or getting a strategy together. Jemma looked at Carl. 'I'm sorry this hasn't been quite the leaving do we planned.'

Carl shrugged. 'It was great until they turned up.' He glanced at his watch. 'I'd better go; Mum's cooking my favourite, and she said I'd better not be late.' He mimed holding a phone to his ear. 'I'll call you.'

***

Thoughts chased each other round Jemma's head as she walked the short distance to The Friendly Bookshop and let herself into her flat. She jumped as Folio ran between her legs. 'What are you doing up here?'

'Meow,' said Folio.

'Never mind that,' said Jemma. 'Raphael needs you, so I suggest you get yourself back to the shop.' She followed him downstairs and opened the main door for him. He trotted down the street, the tip of his tail twitching. *I'd better check on Luna.*

She went into the shop, switched on the light, and looked for the cat. Not in the box with the blanket. Not eating. Not behind the counter. Not under a shelf, or on top of a shelf. Not in the stockroom.

'Luna!' There was no answering squeak.

Maybe she's gone for a wander. She had left a back window locked slightly open. *She will return, won't she?* She sighed. *In any case, there's nothing I can do.*

Her stomach rumbled. *That's something I can fix.* She went upstairs, checked all the rooms in the flat, and made herself a bowl of cheesy pasta. Then she flicked the TV on and watched a few minutes of a panel show while she ate, but it didn't hold her attention. Setting her bowl aside, she fetched a notepad and began a mind map of everything to do regarding the bookshop. *Compulsory purchase order – find out about. Consultation meetings – get dates, make a list of questions, organise attendance. Banners – agree wording, get printed. Can we organise awareness events? Badges?*

After half an hour of writing absolutely everything she could think of, she had a disorganised jumble which hurt her head. *I give up.* She made a cup of tea, picked up her book from the coffee table, and went up the short flight of stairs to her bedroom.

A pair of green eyes glowed in the light from the landing, and Luna squeaked from the centre of the bed.

'You weren't here before,' said Jemma. 'Did Folio sneak you in?'

Luna walked to the end of the bed, accepted a stroke, then strolled back and plumped herself down in exactly the same spot.

'You've got a box downstairs,' said Jemma. 'I'm not at all sure you should be sleeping on the bed.'

Luna put her head on her paws.

'I'm getting into my pyjamas,' said Jemma, 'and when I've finished, I don't expect you to be here.'

Two minutes later, Luna hadn't moved.

'Fine,' said Jemma. 'You can stay while I read, but when I want to go to bed properly, you'll have to move.' She arranged her pillows, got into bed, switched on the reading lamp, and opened her book.

Jemma opened her eyes to bright winter sunlight. Her book was open face down on the bed and she was curled around something large, round, and warm. She stretched out a careful hand and felt soft fur. 'I'm sure I told you,' she said, and stroked Luna, who responded with a gentle snore.

Chapter 12

'It's nearly time!' squealed Maddy, and turned the radio up, which made both customers in the shop jump.

'Does that have to be so loud?' asked one woman plaintively, as 'Paperback Writer' blared through the shop.

'Raphael will be on the radio in a minute,' said Maddy, proudly. 'He owns this bookshop, you know. He's talking about our campaign to save Burns Books. Have you signed the petition?' Maddy took the customer's arm, led her to the counter, and picked up the clipboard. 'Over a thousand signatures,' she said, 'and that's just in this bookshop. The main bookshop's got loads more. Can I interest you in a badge?' She proffered a navy button badge with *Save Burns Books* in white, an open book beneath, and the website address around the outside. 'You can take one for a friend too, if you like.'

'Ssh,' said Jemma. 'He's on.'

'You're listening to Candy Carr, and our guest today is Raphael Burns, who owns Burns Books on Charing Cross Road,' said the DJ. 'The council has announced an innovative new proposal to build a transport hub, and Mr Burns's bookshop is one of the sites which could potentially be affected.'

'I think you mean demolished,' said Raphael.

'Mmm,' said Candy Carr.

'And it isn't only my shop,' said Raphael. 'All the shops in our parade would disappear, and local traders who have been here for many years would have to find new homes for their businesses.'

'But don't you agree that reducing congestion and pollution is a good thing?' Jemma could almost hear the DJ leaning forward.

'I'm not denying that what the council are suggesting sounds attractive,' said Raphael. 'However, other sites are nearby, already cleared, which would be just as good for the hub.'

'I take your point, Mr Burns,' said Candy Carr. 'However, when Ronnie Bunce from Westminster Council came in on Monday, he revealed that your parade of shops is the midpoint between three underground stations, and therefore the most cost-effective place for the new hub. We must think of the taxpayers.'

Maddy winced. 'I thought Candy Carr would be on our side. Doesn't she host the Wednesday evening book club?'

'We must also think of the culture and heritage of the area,' said Raphael. 'Rolando's café and delicatessen has been serving customers in the area for at least thirty years, and my own shop, Burns Books, has been here for well over a hundred.'

Candy Carr laughed. 'Presumably you haven't run it all that time, Mr Burns!'

There was a distinct pause. 'I hope I don't look quite that old,' said Raphael.

'Before I put on the next track,' Candy said, hastily, 'do you have a final message for our listeners?'

'Absolutely,' said Raphael. 'We must use our local shops or they will fade away. I understand the appeal of a shiny new transport hub, but please weigh up the value of your community when you respond to the consultation. Otherwise we shall have the best local transport network in the country, but nowhere worth travelling to.'

'Well, that was pretty sombre,' said Candy Carr. 'Thank you for joining us, Mr Burns. Here's Rod Stewart singing "Downtown Train".'

Maddy punched the off button in disgust. 'That DJ definitely supported the hub,' she said. 'I thought the media wasn't meant to be biased.'

'She let Raphael make his point,' said Jemma. 'I just wish he'd remember to mention the website.' She shrugged. 'Anyway, it's done now.'

She felt as if she had spent every waking moment on the campaign: setting up the website, organising banners, phoning up radio stations and newspapers to ask for an interview or find out where to send a press release. Maddy, meanwhile, had taken on most of the work of the bookshop. Jemma knew she must have served a customer or two that week, but had no recollection of doing so.

'They say all publicity is good publicity,' Maddy said, but she didn't sound as if she believed it.

'True,' said Jemma. She glanced at the clock. 'Don't you want to go for lunch?'

Maddy grinned. 'I wouldn't mind,' she said, 'but didn't we agree I'd cover the shop while you chaired that management meeting?'

Jemma clapped a hand to her mouth. 'I'd completely forgotten! And it starts in ten minutes!' She dashed into the back room and put the kettle on. 'Where did I put my notes?'

'What notes?' asked Maddy. Then she grinned. 'Do you mean the bundle of paper you brought down this morning and shoved in the drawer?'

'Yes!' said Jemma, wrenching the drawer open and retrieving several sheets of closely scribbled A4 paper. 'You're a lifesaver.'

'You can thank me later,' said Maddy, as Jemma dashed out.

***

Why did I agree to this? Jemma asked herself, as she squidged the teabag against the side of her mug.

Because Raphael caught you unawares and you felt too guilty about the bookshop to say no.

She huffed, and fetched the milk from the fridge. *At least the campaign has stopped me worrying about it, I suppose.* She had spent a half hour here and there scribbling down what she could remember from the management literature she had read. The result wasn't encouraging. *I'll be the sort of chairperson who asks for*

everyone else's views, and then I can sum those up. I hope.
She closed the fridge door, picked up her mug and bundle
of papers, and proceeded carefully upstairs.

Her cup swayed dangerously when Luna shot past her,
squeaking with excitement. 'I'm not feeding you,' said
Jemma, ramming the papers under her arm and fishing for
her keyring. She let herself in, sat at the dining table, and
switched on her laptop. Four minutes to spare. She allowed
herself to breathe. *Calm thoughts, Jemma, calm thoughts.*
She peered at her partial reflection in the screen. *My hair!*
She ran up to the bedroom, threatened it with a hairbrush,
put on lipstick, and dashed back down.

I'll start the meeting bang on time, she thought, and
pulled up the agenda. No apologies had been received
beforehand. *Drusilla will probably look immaculate.* She
wished she had had time to change into something a little
more formal. *Could I...?* But the clock said one minute to
go. She couldn't possibly be late for the first meeting, not
when she was chairing it. She took a few deep breaths, had
a reviving sip of tea, and clicked on *Start Meeting.*

Almost immediately, five faces appeared on the screen.
She recognised Nina's winged glasses and Alice band, but
the rest were unknown to her. 'Hello, everyone,' she said.
'Welcome to today's Management Strategies meeting. My
name is Jemma James, and I have been asked to chair this
group.' She considered adding 'for the time being', but
decided that was rather negative. 'We have two people still
to join, so I'll give it a couple more minutes.' *Is Drusilla
trying to psych me out by being late?*

Nina smiled. 'You needn't wait for Percy,' she said.

'He's always at least ten minutes late, and he has a different excuse every time. My favourite was when his cat had fallen asleep on his laptop, so he couldn't join until she woke up.'

'And then there was the time when he'd been told he couldn't put his computer password on a sticky note on his laptop,' said a middle-aged, bespectacled man in a three-piece suit and bow tie. 'So he moved the sticky note to a secure location and couldn't remember where it was.'

'Or the time when he wasn't late, but he was on a bus, and all the other passengers kept joining in.' A woman about Jemma's age with a string of shocking-pink beads and a polka-dot top giggled. 'And his connection broke every time the bus went under a bridge.'

'So what you're saying is that I probably shouldn't wait,' said Jemma. Various nods and grins. 'Has anyone heard from Drusilla?'

'I thought it was quiet in here,' said Nina. 'That's odd: she's normally first in.'

'I'll check,' said Jemma, hoping against hope. Sure enough, at the top of her inbox was an unopened email from Drusilla Davenport, headed *Meeting Apologies*. She opened the email.

Dear Jemma,

So sorry to miss your debut, but I have been unavoidably detained and I'm afraid I shall not be able to log into the meeting today. Many apologies for the late notice.

Yours sincerely,

Drusilla Davenport, MA
Assistant Keeper, Berkshire

'Tell me what you read and I'll tell you who you are' –
François Mauriac

Jemma switched screens and looked at the faces regarding her. 'Drusilla has sent her apologies, and she won't be joining us today.'

Was she mistaken, or did the five sets of shoulders facing her relax a little? 'Never mind,' said Nina cheerfully. 'I'm sure we can manage.'

'I'm sure we can,' said Jemma. 'Is everyone happy to agree the minutes of the last meeting?' Nods. 'Excellent. In that case, let's move on to the first item.' She couldn't help grimacing as she read *Disciplinary and Punitive Measures*. Then a ray of hope dawned. 'I see Drusilla's name is against this, so I propose we postpone this item until she is here to present it.'

'Oh good,' said Pink Beads Woman, whose screen name appeared to be Jane Austen's Worst Nightmare. 'I was dreading this. I don't think Drusilla would actually advocate the death penalty for misbehaving staff, but she's definitely more a stick than a carrot sort of person.'

'Personally, I'd much rather talk about carrots,' said Jemma. 'Is there a reward scheme?'

Everyone looked thoughtful. 'Do you know,' said Nina, 'there isn't. It's been discussed, but it never comes to anything.'

Just then an extra square popped up and Percy's

forehead was visible. 'Terribly sorry I'm late,' he said.

'Hello, Percy,' said Jemma, trying not to smile too broadly. 'You're a bit, um, low.'

'Am I? Oh dear. Someone must have changed the settings on my chair. Hang on a minute.' A vigorous pumping sound was heard as Percy slowly rose into view. 'That's better. As I was saying, sorry to be late, but I managed to lock myself out of my office again…'

***

'I think we've covered everything,' said Jemma. 'Was that OK?'

'Oh yes,' said Pink Beads Woman, whose real name had turned out to be Hermione Dawes. 'I usually end these meetings feeling lazy, guilty, or positively criminal, so today was a nice change. Do we have to tell Drusilla when the next meeting is? It's so restful without her.'

'We should,' said Jemma, 'but we have a nice positive agenda for next time. Is everyone clear on their action points?'

'Oh, absolutely,' said Three-Piece Suit, or Jeff. 'I shall enjoy researching reward schemes.'

'And I'll think about how we can tie that into our social programme,' said Nina. 'Aren't you joining that committee, Jemma?'

'I am,' said Jemma, 'so that's a good opportunity for joint working.' She glanced at her watch. 'That's an hour, and I must admit I'm starving, so we'll end there. It's been lovely to meet you all, and I'll see you next month, if not before.' There was a chorus of goodbyes as she ended the meeting.

Luna looked up from the windowsill, where she was washing a paw. 'Did you enjoy that?' asked Jemma.

Luna gave her a green-eyed stare, spread her toes wide, and began to clean between them.

Jemma closed the laptop, stroked Luna, then took her empty mug and her lunch downstairs. 'All OK in the shop?' she asked Maddy. 'You can head off if you like.'

But before Maddy could reply, the shop telephone rang. Maddy picked up the receiver. 'Hello, The Friendly Bookshop.' She listened for a moment, then held the phone out to Jemma. 'I think it's for you. He keeps saying Raphael isn't there.'

Jemma crossed the room and took the phone. 'Hello, Jemma James speaking.'

'Oh good,' said an agitated male voice. 'At least, I hope so. I called Burns Books, but Raphael's out, and they said you were his deputy.'

Jemma felt her good mood dribble away. 'Yes, that's right,' she said. 'May I ask who is calling?'

'Sorry, this is Jasper Bantam from the London Library. We've got a bit of a problem.'

Jemma hoped this wasn't a classic British understatement. 'What sort of a problem?'

'Things have got rather out of control—'

'Is this a knowledge emergency?' asked Jemma, crossing her fingers.

There was an audible swallow on the other end of the line. 'I'm afraid so. And I think it might be a Grade Two.'

'A Grade Two?' cried Jemma. *I can't deal with a Grade Two! I've only got as far as a Grade Four and Using a*

Pencil of Truth!

'Look, please can you help me?' Now Jemma could hear shouting and shrieks in the background of the call, and a sound like hundreds of books snapping shut over and over again.

Jemma took a deep breath, opened the cupboard under the counter, and grabbed the knowledge-emergency kitbag. 'I'll be there as soon as I can.'

Chapter 13

Jemma stood outside The Friendly Bookshop, shading her eyes against the bright sunlight, looking for a cab. Of course, on today of all days, none were to be seen. 'Typical,' she muttered, typed *London Library* into her phone, and set off at a fast walk. *I bet the minute I start moving two will come along*, she thought, but she was wrong. When she finally saw a cab, its light was off. And by then, according to the app, she was less than three minutes away. Jemma broke into a run though she knew it was unwise; she would need all her strength to deal with whatever awaited her.

Maddy had turned even paler than usual when Jemma explained what was going on. 'A Grade Two knowledge emergency?'

'*He* thinks it's a Grade Two,' said Jemma. 'Hopefully it's a Grade Three, or better still a Four. Anyway, I don't have much choice. If it's really bad, we'll have to evacuate and try Raphael again.' She paused. 'Does anyone know where Raphael is?'

Maddy shook her head. 'I'm not sure you should go, Jemma.'

'I can't not go,' said Jemma. 'I'm the Assistant Keeper. I'll call you as soon as I can, OK?'

'Make sure you do,' said Maddy, looking more troubled than Jemma had ever seen her.

'Your destination is straight ahead,' the app intoned.

Gosh, really? thought Jemma, slowing down a touch as she took in the tall, imposing facade. *No time to appreciate that now*, she told herself. *You've got work to do.*

She ran up the steps and into the building, and was reassured by the cheerful pink carpet and warm wood shelving. Surely nothing too bad could happen somewhere with a pink carpet.

'Can I help you?' The speaker was a small woman in a neat blouse, sitting at a large, curved wooden desk with bookshelves behind her. She might have been there for all eternity.

'Where's the emergency?' said Jemma. Only then did she realise she wasn't out of breath, despite her run. Perhaps being an Assistant Keeper had its advantages.

'Are you a member?' the woman asked.

'What? No, I'm the Assistant Keeper for Westminster. Jasper phoned about the knowledge emergency.' Jemma unslung the kitbag from her shoulder and held it up.

'Not a member...' The woman seemed to have difficulty processing this. 'I'm sorry, but nobody may enter the library without showing their membership card.'

'Oh, for heaven's sake.' Jemma pulled out her phone, navigated to recent calls, and pressed the last number. It rang five times before Jasper answered. 'Yes?' he gasped.

'It's Jemma, I've just arrived. Where are you?'

'The reading room, on the first floor. Come quickly! We're trapped!'

'Phones are only allowed on the sixth floor,' the woman said crossly. 'And that bag needs to go in a locker—' But Jemma had spotted a flight of stairs and was already on her way. The stairs were covered in the same pink carpet, and the banister was solid and reassuring, but she quailed as she raced up the steps. *What shall I find?*

She came to a door. *Jasper says they're trapped; I'll have to break this down.* Jemma took a few steps back then ran at the door, left shoulder forward, expecting to crash against it. *What sort of idiot runs at a locked door,* she thought, as she sailed through and almost ran into a table.

'Which one of you is Jasper Bantam?' she asked the terrified people huddled by the back wall.

A tall skinny blond man in a dark suit, who reminded her of a much better-dressed Raphael, raised a tentative hand. 'That would be me,' he said. 'How did you do that?'

'I, um, opened the door,' said Jemma. 'It wasn't difficult. See?' But when she tugged the handle of the door she had come through, it wouldn't budge.

'Oh no, now you're stuck in here too!' exclaimed Jasper. 'Oh dear, I am sorry. And I'm forgetting my manners.' He advanced towards her and held out his hand, which Jemma gripped and shook firmly, more to convince herself than him.

'Jemma James, Assistant Keeper for Westminster,' she said, rather louder than necessary. It might help to reassure the stranded readers, and hopefully inform whatever was causing this that authority had arrived. 'What's the problem?'

'It's up there.' Jasper Bantam pointed to a set of shelves on the far wall, accessible via a metal staircase and walkway. 'I think it's coming from the middle.'

Jemma put down the kitbag and surveyed the area. The shelves at either end of the walkway appeared normal, but the further towards the middle she looked, the more the shelves blurred, as if she were peering through a heat haze. She felt a tiny vibration under her feet, and when she glanced at the shelves again, they appeared darker. The air itself seemed polluted, and the darkness was slowly rising to the ceiling.

'That snapping I heard earlier on the phone...' she said. 'It's stopped.'

'Yes. There were people on the walkway,' said Jasper. 'I moved everyone to the far end of the room and that seemed to calm it. I hoped everything would settle, and it has a little, but I don't like that at all.' He pointed at the ceiling, where the spherical white lights had become a dirty cream colour. 'I think it's spreading.'

'OK,' said Jemma. She crouched and searched through the bag. 'Have you put any new books on the shelves in that area?'

'Not that I can remember,' said Jasper. 'It's possible another staff member has. Or one of our readers could

105

have put something back in the wrong place.'

'Oh yes, that happens a lot,' said Jemma. 'I work in a bookshop, and we're always re-shelving things.'

'A bookshop, you say?' Jasper Bantam looked startled. 'If you don't mind me saying so, you seem rather young for an Assistant Keeper.'

'Mmm,' said Jemma. She pulled a large white handkerchief from the kitbag and tied it over her nose and mouth. Whatever the book – or books – were emitting, she was pretty sure she didn't want to breathe it in. Next she located a pair of leather gauntlets and pulled them on. She drew out the metal book tongs and snapped them experimentally a couple of times, which provoked reciprocal snapping from the far bookshelf.

'Please don't do that,' Jasper murmured nervously.

'Sorry,' said Jemma. She rooted in the bag again and her hands closed on a box slightly larger than a paperback book. 'Darn,' she said. 'If I'd thought, I'd have packed the bigger one.' She opened the box and scrutinised the lead lining. 'Let's hope it's a small one, eh?' She pushed her hair out of her eyes and walked slowly towards the bookcase.

'Be careful!' cried a shrill voice. Jemma raised the box in acknowledgement and carried on. She didn't dare glance behind her in case something took her by surprise.

She tucked the box under her arm and reached for the handrail of the stairs. The higher she climbed the warmer the handrail grew, even through the gauntlet, until she had to let go. The walkway trembled, and the air felt stale and thin.

'I can't look,' someone said.

'Neither can I,' said a male voice. 'But there's really interesting research to be done on the observable physical effects of paranormal phenomena.'

'Not now, Bernard,' the first voice said, irritably.

Jemma inched along the walkway, careful not to touch the rail, feeling the floor shudder beneath her. The heat was coming up through the soles of her shoes. She wiped her sweaty brow with her forearm. 'I am an Assistant Keeper,' she muttered. *You can do better than that.* 'I am the Assistant Keeper for Westminster.'

The juddering paused, as if the walkway were listening.

'I am the Assistant Keeper for Westminster, and I want you to stop this.' She breathed in, made a face at the disgusting taste in her mouth, and coughed. When she opened her eyes, a golden spark drifted past her.

'Watch out!' cried Jasper.

Whatever you're going to do, Jemma told herself, *get on with it. You haven't much time.*

The air was darkening and smoke-filled, almost oily. Jemma turned away, took a deep breath, then focused on the bookshelf. The smoke was thickest on the fourth shelf from the ceiling, which was just below her eye level. She bent and scrutinised the books. *If I take them out...* But they were so closely packed that the tongs did nothing, and neither did the thick fingers of the gauntlet. Jemma wrenched off the glove, clenched her teeth, and pulled the central book from the shelf. It hit the floor with a sound like a thunderclap.

There was a collective gasp behind her, but the shelf

shook harder. *Concentrate, Jemma.*

A wisp of grey smoke curled upwards from the spine of a small black volume.

'I am the Assistant Keeper for Westminster,' Jemma told it.

The book sent up a longer, darker plume.

'Right, if that's how it is…' Jemma grabbed the book, gritting her teeth not to cry out at the heat, fitted it into the lead-lined box, and closed the lid. The box jerked in her hands, and it was all she could do to hold it closed. In the end she put the box on the walkway, planted her foot on it, and fastened the catch.

The box shook once, twice, a third time . . . and was still.

Jemma bent, picked up the box, and walked slowly along the walkway and down the steps. She felt utterly drained. A small ripple of applause began; already the air was fresher, and the stinging sensation from the searing-hot book was leaving her fingers.

She walked towards Jasper, who took an involuntary step back before collecting himself and stepping forward to meet her. 'It looks like this was the problem,' she said. 'I didn't manage to see which book it was, but I suggest I take it with me.'

'Oh,' said Jasper. 'The thing is, we don't tend to let books leave the library.'

'I had a feeling you'd say that,' Jemma replied. 'In that case, I can let it out and be on my way—'

'No, no, I didn't mean that,' said Jasper. 'I'm sure a temporary loan would be perfectly in order.' He ran a finger around the back of his collar. 'Do you know, I might open a window. It is rather stuffy in here.'

Someone giggled, and before long everyone in the room was smiling, laughing, miming gasping for air, and pointing to the now clearly visible bookshelf.

Jasper went to the door and gave it a tentative pull. It opened as if it had never given any trouble at all. 'It looks as if we have normality.' The members collected their papers, paraphernalia and transparent bags then wandered out, talking animatedly, gesturing at the bookshelf, and casting shy glances at Jemma.

Jasper pumped her hand warmly. 'I can't thank you enough,' he said. 'I've never seen anything like that. What happened?'

Jemma shook her head. 'I suspect the book was either in the wrong place, or too close to another powerful book,' she said. 'But this one was definitely the troublemaker. I'll take it to the bookshop, examine it in a calm atmosphere, and let you know what I find. But that might have to wait until Raphael returns.'

'Of course, yes, I quite understand.' Jasper collected the stray items of Jemma's emergency kit, gave them back to her, and held the door open. 'Thank you so much for coming, Jemma.'

Jemma smiled, then realised she still had a handkerchief over half her face and untied it. 'That's quite all right, although I did wonder if your receptionist would let me in. I'm not a member, you see.'

Comprehension dawned on Jasper's face. He escorted Jemma to the front desk, had a word with the woman, who appeared outraged, and handed Jemma a small plastic card. 'You could always come here for research too, of course.' He looked rather shy. 'Do you have a business card? Just in case I need – I mean, the library ever needs you again.'

Jemma rooted in the kitbag, found a battered card, and handed it to him. 'There you go,' she said. 'Hopefully the next time we meet won't be at another knowledge emergency.' Her stomach rumbled threateningly. 'Anyway,' she said, hastily, 'I'd better get back to the shop. My assistant hasn't had her lunch yet.' She raised a hand in farewell to Jasper, waved to the still-outraged receptionist, and walked down the steps of the London Library at a much slower pace than she had entered it.

Chapter 14

'You're absolutely sure you're OK?' Maddy asked, for perhaps the third time.

Jemma laughed. 'I'm absolutely fine,' she said. 'To be honest, I don't think it was a Grade Two. I didn't tell Jasper Bantam that, obviously.'

'Obviously.' Maddy eyed the kitbag. 'Could I – could I see it?'

'You must be joking,' said Jemma. 'There's no way I'm letting it out until Raphael is back to supervise.'

'Because it really wasn't that serious,' said Maddy. 'What shall we do with it? Are you putting it in the stockroom?'

'Good question,' said Jemma. 'I think the best thing to do is take it to Burns Books and put it in the stockroom there. For one thing, there's more room, so I can keep it away from anything likely to set it off.' She gave Maddy a guilty look.

Maddy rolled her eyes. 'Off you go. It's a good thing I brought a salad in this morning. Although Luna's cross that I stole a tin of her salmon.' Luna was sitting with her nose in the air and her back to Maddy. 'I think she's making a point.'

'That wouldn't surprise me in the slightest,' said Jemma. 'OK, I'll try not to be too long. I might pick up a panini while I'm over there, if they've got any left.' She put the kitbag on her shoulder, tickled Luna's chin, and left the shop.

'Hi there,' she said to Luke, who was having a quick swig from his drinks bottle. 'I don't suppose Raphael's back yet?'

Luke wiped his mouth and put the bottle under the counter. 'Not yet, no. Why, do you need him?'

'Sort of.' Jemma held up the kitbag. 'I've got a misbehaving book in here and I'd like Raphael to have a look at it. I wondered if I could put it in the stockroom.'

'A misbehaving book, eh?' said Luke. 'What has it been doing?'

'Terrorising the patrons of the London Library,' said Jemma, casually. 'Grade Two knowledge emergency.'

Luke's eyes widened. 'I have no idea what that means, but it sounds serious.' He surveyed the bookshelves. The ground floor was quiet, with only a couple of customers browsing in Self-Help and Art. 'You brought it with you?'

'Yes. It's in a lead-lined box, so it should be secure.' Jemma opened the bag and removed the box.

'It doesn't seem particularly dangerous,' said Luke,

peering at it.

'Before I got there, it was snapping at people,' said Jemma. 'And it was doing something to the air.'

Luke gave the box a nervous glance. 'I'm not sure I want to know.'

'If you're worried, I could put an extra restraint on it.' Jemma opened a drawer in the counter and pulled out a thin silver chain and a tiny padlock. She wound the chain round the box as if tying up a parcel, and secured it with the padlock. 'There, that should hold it. Anyway, it seems calm now. Perhaps it's tired.'

Luke followed her through to the stockroom. Jemma gazed at the shelves, seeking somewhere suitable for the book. 'Have you been reorganising in here? It looks different.'

'Might have been,' said Luke. 'Maddy keeps your stockroom so neat, and I wanted ours to be a bit less chaotic.'

'Were there any books that Raphael told you not to move?'

Luke pointed to the furthest aisle. 'He said that as long as I didn't disturb anything there, it was fine.'

'Good.' Jemma walked down the aisle nearest to her, found a space, and slid the box into it. There was no resistance from the book, no warmth, and no reaction from any of the books around it. 'I think that'll do.' She pulled out her phone and texted Raphael: *Dealt with knowledge emergency and brought culprit to BB. Currently chained in box and shelved in*— 'What section is this?' she asked.

'Miscellaneous,' said Luke. 'It all is. It may seem neat,

but I've completely given up trying to classify anything.'

'OK.' Jemma went back to her text: *...the aisle nearest the door, away from any other dangerous books. Would appreciate your opinion when you return.*

She stepped back and looked at the box, then touched it. The box was still and quiet, and at the same temperature as its surroundings. She let out a breath. Perhaps this was how bomb disposal experts felt.

'We're good,' she said. 'While I'm here, I'll pop down for a coffee and a bite to eat. I haven't got as far as lunch.'

'You might as well make it afternoon tea,' said Luke. 'Go and see what the vultures have left you.'

'Always the optimist,' said Jemma, with a grin, and headed for the stairs.

For a wonder, there was no queue in the café, and plenty of tables free. Jemma approached the display case.

'Hi Jemma, what can I get you?' Em was wearing a Rolando's apron, and Jemma had to admit that she seemed very much at home.

'Can I have – can you do a cappuccino?'

'I can do a cappuccino,' said Em. 'Anything with that?'

'And a tuna melt, please.' Jemma looked longingly at the various cakes and pastries in the cabinet. *Maybe later.*

'Coming up,' said Em. She took the tuna melt from the display and put it in the warmer, then turned to the coffee machine and began manipulating levers.

'Has it been quiet today?' said Jemma.

Em considered. 'We had the usual rush at lunchtime, but otherwise, yes, I suppose it has. For here, anyway.' She smiled at Jemma over her shoulder. 'It's certainly a change from working in an open-plan office.'

'Isn't it,' said Jemma.

'So did you just pop in for a brew?' asked Em. 'Not that it's any of my business—'

'I was delivering a book,' said Jemma. 'It's one Raphael might take a particular interest in.' She considered how much she could say without giving anything away about the shop, or indeed, her position in it. 'It's on loan to us from the London Library.'

'You've got a book from a library?' said Em. 'Isn't that quite unusual?'

'I suppose it is,' said Jemma, 'but Raphael has – expertise – on certain books. I'm learning a bit, too.'

'You've really got into it,' said Em, as the warmer beeped. She removed the tuna melt, inspected it with a critical eye, then put a napkin-wrapped knife and fork on the side of the plate. 'I'll just finish your cappuccino.' She made the drink, then picked up the cocoa powder and a piece of plastic. Holding the plastic over the drink, she shook on cocoa powder. 'There you go.' She put the cup on the counter, and Jemma saw the letters *BB* on top of her drink.

'That's clever,' she said.

'Same idea as a stencil,' said Em. 'The customers seem to like it.'

'They do,' said a voice behind Jemma, and she turned to see a stout man in a navy-blue business suit. 'Hi, Em, the usual, please.'

'Coming up, Edwin,' said Em. 'Drink in or take away?'

Edwin made a face. 'Better take it away, I suppose.

Work to do.' He leaned on the counter. 'I don't know what I'll do when this place goes.'

Jemma wheeled round. 'What do you mean, when this place goes? We're not going anywhere.'

'The *Courier* says you are,' said Edwin. 'Not you specifically, but this whole parade is getting demolished. It was in this morning's paper.' He went over to the rack by the till and collected a copy. 'Look.' He opened the paper and riffled through it. 'I knew I'd seen it. Page five.'

SITE CHOSEN FOR NEW TRANSPORT HUB, read Jemma.

A dramatic new development in the ongoing saga of the new Charing Cross transport hub has reduced the number of feasible options to one – and that one is a parade of six shops including Burns Books, which has mounted a feisty campaign against its closure.

DZD Holdings, which is working with Westminster Council on the construction of the transport hub, announced today that surveys of the three potential development sites have revealed that two sites have problems with bedrock and subsidence which rule them out of consideration. 'It's unfortunate,' said a spokesperson, 'but it appears we have no choice.'

While public consultation is still ongoing, feedback so far has been that the public are overwhelmingly in favour of the new hub. Our reporter spoke to some of the parade's shopkeepers and staff, and gained the following feedback from a source who did not wish to be identified:

'Personally, I think it's a good thing. These buildings

116

are old-fashioned, antiquated, barely fit for purpose. We must move with the times and take this area into the twenty-first century. Let's face it, most people buy their books from Amazon anyway.'

Other sources were less keen on the development, it must be said, but as Westminster Council are issuing a compulsory purchase order, it seems their objections will be in vain.

'See,' said Edwin, tapping the paper. 'Unfortunately, I don't think anything can be done now.'

'I'm not giving up without a fight,' Jemma replied. She looked at Em, who was biting her lip. 'You agree, don't you, Em?'

Em jumped. 'Yes, yes of course.' She rubbed her forehead as if she had a headache. 'I'm sorry, Edwin, what was it you wanted again?'

'The usual,' said Edwin, with a smile. 'This has really got to you, hasn't it?'

Jemma considered asking for a takeaway cup and heading to The Friendly Bookshop, but something stopped her. She sat down at a nearby table facing the counter and studied Em under cover of rereading the article in the *Courier*. Was it her imagination, or did Em look guilty? *A source who did not wish to be identified...* Every so often Em glanced in her direction and Jemma hastily turned a page of the paper, though she saw nothing, and the tuna melt might as well have been made of cardboard.

She considered phoning the *Courier* offices, getting hold of that reporter, and asking point-blank whom they had spoken to . . . but that would do no good. Anyway, who else would have said such things? Certainly some of the shopkeepers, particularly those who owned their premises, were in favour of the hub, but which of them would have mentioned books? Jemma took a sip of her cappuccino and watched Em over the rim of the cup. *I don't know what you're up to, but whatever it is, you won't win.*

Chapter 15

Over breakfast on Friday, Jemma reread the newspaper headline with a sigh of satisfaction.

COUNCIL PLAN TO BULLDOZE LOCAL SHOPS
Owners last to know

She had managed to persuade Carl to visit the *Courier* offices with her an hour before they put the paper to bed. 'It's not that I don't support the campaign,' he had said. 'But I don't see myself as a talking head. And I'm due at the arts centre in ninety minutes.'

'Like it or not, you're a name now,' said Jemma, giving his arm a pat. 'You're the most sort-of-famous person we've got. I'm fully prepared to use that to our advantage.'

Carl sighed. 'OK. Just let me get my ad libs organised.' To be fair, he had given a great performance to the reporter, with exactly the right levels of dignity, confusion, and community spirit. The reporter had used his words more or less as they stood.

'You don't think we're throwing too much at this, do you?' he had asked, once they were safely clear of the offices.

'I'm throwing everything at it,' said Jemma. 'Especially as Raphael hasn't had any luck.'

When Raphael had eventually returned to Burns Books, just as Jemma was preparing to leave for The Friendly Bookshop, he had been so downcast that Jemma had asked him what was wrong in front of Em.

'Espresso, please, Em,' Raphael had said before answering her. 'I've been in meetings with Armand Dupont.'

'In Paris?' murmured Jemma, her eyebrows halfway up her forehead.

'Naturellement,' said Raphael. 'I can hardly talk about it here, can I?'

Jemma looked around her. While the bookshop wasn't showing any visible signs of distress – no rumbling, no falling books, no flickering lights – the air felt thin and it was cooler than usual. 'What did he say?'

Raphael sighed. 'More or less what I thought he would. While he is sympathetic, and ready to help financially in any way he can, it would be impossible for him to take any direct action to keep the shop open.'

'Excuse me?' Em stood two feet away, holding an espresso cup. 'I'm sorry, but I couldn't help hearing. I thought you owned the shop, Raphael. Who is Armand

Dupont?'

'It's complicated,' said Jemma.

'He's a sort of investor,' said Raphael. 'And while he is very powerful in the right circles, his power is limited.'

'I suppose it would be,' said Em. 'Here's your espresso, anyway.' She looked at Jemma. 'Will you tell Raphael, or shall I?'

'Oh no.' Raphael took the cup, drained it, then handed it to Em. 'I should have asked for a double. Go on, tell me the worst.'

'Apparently the developers have done a survey and our site is the only one that will work.' said Jemma. 'And the consultation so far says the public want the transport hub.'

'Ouch,' said Raphael.

'It must be terrible for you,' said Em, as she walked back to the coffee machine, 'but you can always open another bookshop. I mean, it's really busy here, the shop's doing well, and you've got lots of customers. I'm sure they would move with you.'

'That isn't the point,' said Raphael. 'It isn't just about the location, you see, I— *Ow!*'

'Oh sorry,' said Jemma. 'I didn't see your foot there.' Once Em was safely turned away, she shook her head with a warning expression and mouthed *Don't tell her*. Raphael raised his eyebrows, but said nothing.

Em delivered the second espresso. 'So what is this about, then, if it isn't the location?'

'Oh, you know,' said Raphael vaguely. 'It's such a nice building.' He gestured around him at the brickwork, the arches, and the stone floor. 'The shop's been in the family

121

a long time. It practically *is* family.'

'Mmm,' said Em. 'If you don't mind, I might finish early today. The shop's quiet, and I've got time owing.'

'Why not,' said Raphael. He took his espresso to a table, sat down, and ran his hands through his hair with the air of a man carrying the world on his shoulders. Jemma considered objecting to Em's request on the grounds that the café usually wouldn't close for another ninety minutes, but decided that would be churlish. Anyway, what could Em do? The way things were going, the council and the public would stitch up the bookshop between them without any additional help from her…

Jemma's breakfast reverie was rudely interrupted by her mobile ringing. It was the ringtone she had assigned to Em: 'Ding Dong! The Witch Is Dead.' She looked at the phone, debating whether to answer it or not. On one hand, today's newspaper had put her in a good mood and she didn't want to spoil it. On the other, if Em were up to something, better that she knew about it. Curiosity won the day. 'Hi,' she said. 'Let me guess, you'll be late in.'

'I've had an idea,' said Em. 'I haven't said anything to Raphael yet – I'd rather not get his hopes up – but I think this could work.'

Jemma eyed her uneaten slice of toast. 'What could work?'

'It was something Raphael said yesterday about the building being in his family for years and years.'

'And?'

'It looks really old, at least downstairs. Do you know how old it is?'

'Twelfth century or thereabouts,' said Jemma. 'We researched it, and the lower floor of the shop is a crypt from an old cathedral.'

'Yes!' cried Em. 'That's just the thing!'

'Are you going to tell me, or not?'

'Isn't it obvious?'

'No!' snapped Jemma. 'Do get on with it, will you? It's too early in the morning for guessing games.'

'All right,' said Em. 'If the building's that old, surely it ought to be listed. And if it's listed, I'm pretty sure it can't be demolished.'

Clarity whooshed into Jemma's brain. 'Oh my gosh, you're right. At least, you sound right. Have you followed it up?'

'Well,' said Em, 'I looked up getting listed building status, and apparently you only have to fill in a form to get things started. There's even a way to fast-track it. When I say fast track, it takes three months, but according to the project plans I've seen for the transport hub, that would be OK.'

'I see,' said Jemma. 'You've been busy.'

'It did say there was a cost involved with the fast tracking,' said Em, 'but if Raphael's investor is OK with that, it shouldn't be a problem.'

'No,' said Jemma. 'And the people from the council raved about the shop when they came to see it. I bet they'd support our application.'

'Great,' said Em. 'Shall I fill it in, then?'

'Shouldn't you talk to Raphael first? It's his shop. I'm sure he'll be fine with it, but we'd better ask.' She glanced at the clock: ten past eight. 'The best thing to do is wait until Raphael comes down, make sure he's had at least one coffee, and tell him then.'

'I take it you want to be there,' said Em.

'Well, yes,' said Jemma. 'The sooner Raphael gives us the go-ahead, the quicker we can get moving. It's not just the form; this is part of our campaign. I mean, what would the media say about the council trying to bulldoze a piece of history?' She grinned. 'Doesn't bear thinking about.' And she bit into her second piece of toast with relish.

***

By that afternoon, everything was moving along nicely. Em had completed the form with help from Raphael, Jemma, and an outraged member of the council's Heritage Team, it had been submitted to Historic England, and Jemma had sent a press release to every newspaper she could think of. She had also updated the Save Burns Books social media feeds with the latest news and received messages of support from all over the world. A few people had asked whether they could donate to the bookshop, so Jemma had set up a crowdfunding page, and the total was climbing hour by hour. *At this rate*, she thought, *Armand Dupont won't have to put his hand in his pocket at all.*

An emphatic cough from Maddy pulled Jemma back to The Friendly Bookshop. 'I know it's all very exciting,' she said, 'but could you mind the shop while I get teabags? We've run out, and to be honest, I need the caffeine.'

'Yes, of course, Maddy,' said Jemma, guiltily. She grinned. 'It's great, though, isn't it? Finally we're getting somewhere.'

Maddy smiled back. 'Of course it is, although I must admit I'll be glad when it's sorted.' She took a five-pound note from the till. 'I'll get biscuits as well.' She opened the door and Folio dashed in. 'Hello, Folio,' she said. 'I won't ask who you're here to see.'

Folio trotted straight to the basket in the corner, where Luna lay stretched out with her chin on the edge, and touched her nose with his own.

Luna's eyes half opened, then closed again.

Folio stood for a moment, as if debating what to do, then came over to the counter and meowed at Jemma.

'OK, OK!' said Jemma. 'Hang on a minute.' She tore off the top sheet of the notepad, crumpled it into a ball, and dropped it on the floor. Folio picked it up in his mouth, carried it to Luna, and dropped it. Luna's right paw twitched, then she batted the paper ball diagonally across the shop. A moment later she was crouched by her basket, bottom waggling from side to side, ready to pounce.

'I could watch these two for hours,' said Maddy. 'Anyway, tea.'

'I'll brew up when you get back,' said Jemma, smiling. If Folio felt confident enough to leave the shop and come to play with Luna, surely things would be all right. *And I have the last night of Carl's play to look forward to tomorrow...* She giggled as a swipe from Folio sent the ball under a bookcase yet again, and bent to retrieve it. 'Ready?' she asked the cats, holding the ball up. 'Steady... Go!'

Chapter 16

Jemma was in the middle of gift wrapping a book for a customer on Monday when the phone rang. 'Could you get that?' she asked Maddy. 'I'm at a delicate stage.'

'Sure,' said Maddy, hurrying over. 'Good morning, The Friendly Bookshop, how can I help you?' She listened. 'OK, I'll let her know. Bye.'

'Let me know what?' asked Jemma, as she made a neat point at one end of the parcel and folded it into the middle. She found wrapping books therapeutic, when she had the time and wasn't fretting about the shop. *Thank heavens that's finished...*

Maddy watched her make and stick down a second point, then add a ribbon and curl the ends. 'I can go on the till, if you want,' she said.

Jemma glanced at her, then moved to the back of the counter. Maddy followed her. 'Code red,' she said. 'Those two guys have turned up. You know, *those* two guys.'

'I'll head over,' said Jemma. She grabbed her coat and bag, then, for no reason that she could fathom, got the knowledge-emergency kitbag too. 'Hopefully it's nothing.'

Maddy crossed her fingers out of view of the customer, then moved forward. 'So that's seven ninety-nine, please.'

Jemma ran to Burns Books, not sure what she might find. Luke was on the top till dealing with a customer, and while he was chatting in his usual manner she could tell his mind was elsewhere. 'Morning, Luke,' she said.

'Morning, Jemma,' he replied. 'You're wanted downstairs.' The look he gave her spoke volumes.

Mr Bunce and Mr Tipping, still wearing their raincoats even though it was a nice day, stood slightly to one side, waiting for Raphael to finish serving a customer. 'Would you like me to take over?' Jemma murmured to Raphael.

Raphael glanced at Messrs Bunce and Tipping, and his expression was not particularly friendly. 'I'm sure these gentlemen don't mind waiting for a moment,' he said, reaching under the counter for a paper bag. 'There you are, madam, that will be fourteen pounds and ninety-eight pence, please. Cash or card?'

The two men were shifting from foot to foot and Mr Tipping was murmuring to Mr Bunce. Jemma shivered; what might happen if they were kept waiting too long? But then, what could they do? The bookshop was in a better position to resist them than it had ever been – not that they knew it. She looked past them to Em, who was leaning on the café counter in a rare quiet moment, and raised her eyebrows. Em shrugged and continued to watch the men.

Finally the customer went on her way and the two men stepped forward. 'Mr Burns,' said Mr Bunce, removing his hat and handing it to Mr Tipping, 'we have a little something for you. We could have done it electronically, but I prefer to attend to these matters in person.' He reached into the inside pocket of his raincoat and handed Raphael an envelope.

Raphael glanced at it, then him. 'And this would be...?'

A short, mirthless laugh jerked out of Mr Bunce. 'You know perfectly well what this is, Mr Burns. That compulsory purchase order we've been promising you.'

'Ah,' said Raphael. 'I see.' He jumped as Folio leapt onto the counter, tail flicking, and sat down facing the two men. Then he handed the envelope back to Mr Bunce. 'I'm sorry, but this won't be any use.'

'Really?' asked Mr Bunce, eyebrows raised. 'No use, Mr Burns? What makes you say that?'

Raphael's eyes gleamed. 'We've applied for listed building status for the bookshop, and we have allies at the council. So I don't think you'll be able to demolish this place after all. I'm terribly sorry.'

'Oh dear,' said Mr Bunce. 'That's a bit of a surprise, isn't it, Mr Tipping?'

Mr Tipping giggled. 'Oh yes.'

Mr Bunce tapped the letter against his palm. 'I'm impressed that you've gone to so much trouble.'

'You flatter us,' said Raphael. 'It wasn't difficult. I'd have done it years ago if I'd realised how easy it was.'

'I'm sure you would,' said Mr Bunce. 'But that wouldn't have given you your moment of triumph, would it? I mean, talk about pulling it back at the last minute. Eh, Mr Tipping?'

Mr Tipping nodded fervently.

'Since you can't serve us with that order, I imagine you have other things to be getting on with,' said Raphael. 'Unless you'd like to browse the shelves, or have a coffee and a snack…?'

Mr Bunce gazed around the shop. 'It's a tempting offer,' he said, 'and it is getting on for lunchtime.' He turned back to Raphael. 'But I think I *will* serve this order.' He put the envelope on the counter and squared it up.

Raphael eyed it. 'What's the point, Mr Bunce?'

Mr Bunce puffed his chest out. 'The point is, Mr Burns, that one of your chums in the council gave me an earful on Friday and in doing so, let me know exactly what you were up to. So I made a few adjustments.'

Raphael looked uneasy. 'What do you mean?'

The oak door creaked open and Maddy dashed in, accompanied by Luna, who was squeaking as though someone had trodden on her tail. 'What's going on?' Maddy demanded.

Jemma moved to her side. 'What are you doing here?' she murmured.

'Luna has been bristling and squeaking at the shop door for the last five minutes,' said Maddy. 'And I felt – peculiar. When I opened the door, she ran straight to the shop.'

'Another cat, I see,' said Mr Bunce. He bent and inspected Luna, who hissed at him. 'That isn't good for health and safety or the building, is it? Cats doing their business everywhere.'

A distinct rumble sounded beneath their feet. 'And possible subsidence. Oh dear.' Mr Bunce shook his head. 'It's a crying shame when a nice building goes to rack and ruin. Isn't it, Mr Tipping?'

Mr Tipping, who had also been shaking his head, changed quickly to a nod. 'Yes, Mr Bunce.'

'And that's why we're purchasing your building, Mr Burns,' said Mr Bunce, still with that sad note in his voice. 'A wonderful building, not looked after properly – it's a scandal. So we'll buy it and incorporate it into the design of the transport hub, because we can't let somewhere like this go to waste.' With his forefinger, he pushed the letter towards Raphael. 'As you would know if you'd bothered to read my letter.'

'You can't do this,' said Raphael.

Mr Bunce grinned. 'I just did. And as I'm a nice man, I'll tell you that you have twenty-one days to object.' He took his hat from Mr Tipping and put it on. 'Good luck.'

The rumble beneath intensified. Mr Tipping grabbed hold of Mr Bunce, and even Raphael took hold of the counter. 'Don't worry!' he shouted, as customers squealed and grasped shelves and tables. Books plopped on the ground like fat raindrops.

'What's going on?' cried Em. 'What's happening?'

Mr Bunce sucked his teeth. 'You ought to get that looked at, Mr Burns, but it might be a little too late. Come along, Mr Tipping.' He walked to the door, doing his best to go straight.

Luna leapt onto the counter beside Folio. The two cats,

tails fluffed out and sticking upwards, stared hard at the ceiling, where the chandeliers were swinging as if caught in a gale and flickering on and off. Everything seemed jerky, as if it were running at half speed.

'Jemma,' said Raphael, 'can you go upstairs and keep the stockroom door closed? I have to manage things down here.'

'Is there anything I can do?' asked Maddy.

'Yes,' said Raphael. 'Please look after Em and the customers.' She followed his gaze to Em, who was flattened against the back wall of the café, glancing this way and that as though she didn't know where danger might come from.

Carl ran in. 'What's going on? I was passing, and I felt . . . something.' He gazed around him. 'Oh no.'

'I'm afraid so,' said Raphael. 'Can you help Jemma and Luke upstairs? We must stop anyone entering or leaving until this has passed.'

'Right, boss,' said Carl. 'Come on, Jemma, let's sort this.' They dashed upstairs.

'Luke, have you got the key for the stockroom door?' Jemma shouted.

Luke wrenched open the drawer and rummaged. 'I can't see it anywhere.'

Damn. 'OK,' called Jemma. The stockroom door was rattling hard. She gripped the handle tightly and braced herself. Within she could hear things shifting, and the sound of rustling pages. She leaned down to the keyhole. 'I am an Assistant Keeper,' she said. 'I deal with knowledge emergencies.' *I hope it's listening.* 'Please listen, shop,'

131

she pleaded, trying not to panic. 'We're doing our best, we really are.'

'I've bolted the front door,' called Carl. 'I don't know where the key's gone.'

'It's probably with the stockroom key,' Jemma shouted back. *They could be in another dimension for all I know.* She wondered what Raphael was doing downstairs, then shook herself. *Concentrate, Jemma.* 'I am your Assistant Keeper and I want you to calm down. You are Burns Books; you will always be Burns Books. We won't let two men from the council stop that.'

Was she imagining things, or were the door's struggles becoming a little weaker? 'You are a wonderful bookshop, and we won't let anyone change that. You are a very important place.'

The thudding inside the stockroom ceased, and the rustling paused.

'You are the most important bookshop in the country,' Jemma whispered. She took one hand off the handle and stroked the door, which felt warm to the touch. 'We want you to feel better. Raphael is downstairs, and Luke and Carl are looking after the front door. It's going to be all right.'

A little breeze blew through the keyhole, almost like a sigh. The rustling paused, resumed, and paused again. Jemma held her breath, listening, but the stockroom was silent. She exhaled and leaned her forehead against the cooling door, but did not let go of the handle. *Not yet. Not till Raphael says it's safe.* The floor had stopped trembling; she wondered whether it had downstairs, too. *Don't move,*

132

said the voice in her head, and she continued to stroke the stockroom door.

'It seems to have stopped,' called Carl. 'What do we do?'

'One of you stay put,' Jemma replied. 'Maybe one of you could see what's happening downstairs? But be careful.'

'I'll stay here,' said Luke. 'Out of all of us, I know most about not letting unwelcome things over the threshold.'

'Fair point,' said Carl. He came into the back room, put his arms around Jemma in an awkward hug, then went downstairs.

A couple of minutes later, he called, 'All clear. Raphael's sending the customers up.'

Still clutching books, the customers emerged one by one, dazed and blinking. Jemma moved to the counter to help Luke, and five minutes later they had all left the shop. 'I hope they'll come back,' said Luke.

'That's if we have a shop for them to come back to,' said Jemma, and shivered. 'Let's lock up and head downstairs.'

When Jemma opened the great oak door she blinked, then looked again. No, it was still a complete mess. Books lay everywhere: face down on the floor, gathered in heaps in the corners like snowdrifts, draped over the chandeliers like sleeping birds. Chairs and tables were overturned, the heavy brass till had shifted halfway along the counter, and in the café area smashed crockery littered the floor. Folio and Luna lay exhausted on the counter, legs outstretched, their breathing shallow. Raphael was crouched behind it, the palms of his hands flat on the floor. He saw Jemma and straightened up. 'I think we're through the worst,' he said, but there was no hope in his voice.

Luke ran to Maddy, who was at the café counter with Em, and flung his arms around her. Even from this distance, Jemma could see Em shaking. Carl led Em to an armchair and sat her down. 'It's all right, Em. It's over now.'

'It's not all right!' cried Em. 'What the hell just happened? What were the cats doing – what were *you* doing?' She pointed a trembling finger at Raphael.

Raphael leaned against the counter, thoroughly worn out. 'Ah,' he said. 'You see, the bookshop… The bookshop is magical. And I suppose I am, too.'

'All this time, I thought Damon had had a breakdown,' Em said, and her voice had the clenched quality of someone at the end of her tether. 'Either that, or he was making it up. Talking about a trapdoor in the shop, and an underground river, and an octopus in the cellar. I believed he was making excuses for everything going wrong; what was I meant to think? That's why we split up and I returned to London. I couldn't cope with it any more, and I wanted to prove him wrong.'

She rounded on Jemma. 'Why didn't you tell me? You could have warned me when I came, but you didn't. You could have told me at any time, but no. You let me work here, thinking it was a shop like any other, and – and this!' She swept a hand around the wreckage. 'I dumped Damon and came back for this!' Her eyes blazed, then filled with tears, and she buried her head in Carl's shoulder, sobbing.

Chapter 17

Silence hung heavily in the air. Jemma stood rooted to the spot. Eventually, she spoke. 'I didn't know that.'

'What was I supposed to think?' Em's voice was muffled. Then she lifted her head and glared at Jemma.

Jemma shrugged. 'Maybe you and Damon shouldn't have tried to trick us into giving up the shop in the first place. Then none of it would have happened.'

Em dashed her tears away with an impatient hand. 'He told me I had to,' she said, flatly. 'He said it was his big chance, and that if I loved him, I'd help him. As far as I knew this was just some crappy bookshop, and *you*' – she glared even harder – 'were wasting your time trying to turn around a lost cause. As usual.'

Jemma put her hands on her hips and glared back. 'What do you mean, as usual?'

'You know. All the pet projects you stayed late for. All

those reports you wrote that never got read. Seriously, Jemma, if you bet on a race, I'd bet on whoever you chose coming in last.' Em's eyes glittered with malice. 'No, finishing just out of the medals. Working their butt off, but never quite making it.'

Jemma scowled at her. 'That was before I came here. I didn't rate the bookshop until I began to understand it – but why would *you* even bother to try? Miss I'll-Skip-The-Paperwork-And-Coast-Through-The-Meeting. Miss I'll-Talk-My-Way-Out-Of-This. Miss Spreadsheets-Are-For-Losers. You've never worked an extra hour in your life.'

Em's brow furrowed as she looked at Jemma, but her expression was pleading, not angry. 'Of course I said those things – who doesn't?' She sighed. 'OK, not you. Who else is honest about how much time they spend scrambling to keep up?'

Jemma stared at her friend. 'You had me fooled.'

Em studied her feet and an awkward silence fell. 'Sorry,' she muttered.

''S'OK,' Jemma mumbled. She shifted her gaze from Em to the devastation around her. 'Anyway, this won't tidy the bookshop.' She sighed. 'What a mess.'

Raphael surveyed the carnage. 'At least it's still standing,' he said. 'For now.'

Em frowned. 'What were you doing? You put your hands on the floor, and then – then—' She rubbed her eyes. 'It was like an optical illusion.'

'I was holding things together,' said Raphael. 'Carl and Luke were guarding the door, and Jemma was taking care of the stockroom.'

Jemma righted a chair and flopped into it. 'I don't even want to think about the stockroom.' A sudden thought struck her. 'Oh heck, that book.'

The corner of Raphael's mouth lifted. 'Which one? There are several in there to choose from.'

'The one I brought back from the London Library... I texted you, and I meant to tell you in person, but with everything else going on...' Jemma summarised her trip to the library and the trapping and removal of the book.

'Good heavens,' said Raphael. 'Have you filed a report?'

Jemma groaned. 'You never told me there was paperwork.'

''Fraid so,' said Raphael. 'And no, I didn't tell you, because I didn't think you'd be dashing off and rescuing books just yet.' He stood up. 'We should go and check what you have there.'

'Wait a minute,' said Em. 'Does this mean that Jemma is sort of magical too?'

'Of course,' said Raphael. 'How do you think she kept the stockroom door closed? I've got stuff in there that could blow the shop to smithereens if it was in the right mood. Or alternatively, not arranged properly.' He stretched. 'As the shop is still in one piece, I assume we won't find anything too bad.'

They followed him upstairs. Jemma held her breath as he braced himself, then carefully opened the stockroom door. 'So far so good.' He switched on the light.

They looked at the neatly stacked boxes on the shelves. If anything, it appeared slightly tidier than normal.

'Well,' said Raphael. 'This is interesting. Oh, wait a minute.' He pointed at a small chained box lying on the floor of the aisle nearest to them. Every so often, it twitched perhaps a centimetre closer to where they were standing. 'Someone is trying to escape.' He crossed the floor and picked the box up.

'That's the book I brought back,' said Jemma. 'I don't actually know what it is; I was too focused on getting it into the box to open it, and there's nothing on the cover or spine. Luke said your not-to-be-disturbed stuff was on the other side of the stockroom, so I put it as far away from there as possible.'

'Good move. Let's have a look.' Raphael drew a ring of tiny silver keys from his pocket and selected one for the padlock. 'Actually, you should probably all go outside, just in case.'

'Even me?' said Jemma.

'Even you,' Raphael replied. 'I'm sure it'll be fine, but if anything did happen, it would be unwise to have a Keeper and an Assistant Keeper in the room at the same time. Go on, be off with you.'

'Is he serious?' Em asked, as they filed out and walked to the head of the staircase.

Jemma shrugged. 'As far as I know.' She listened. Silence. Then a low mutter: 'Well I'll be—' A few seconds later she heard a quiet, decisive thud and a rattle, followed by a slither as the box was replaced on the shelf.

Raphael left the stockroom, closed the door behind him and gripped the handle firmly. His face was dead white. 'Can someone fetch the key, please,' he said.

138

'We couldn't find it earlier,' Luke faltered.

'Try again,' said Raphael. 'We must lock this room. No one but myself and Jemma is allowed in, do you hear?'

Luke went into the main shop, opened the drawer where the keys were kept and brought it back. 'It was right at the front,' he said, handing it to Raphael. 'It wasn't there earlier, I swear.'

Raphael took the key, rammed it into the lock, and turned it twice. 'I've put the box into a bigger box and put another chain round it,' he said. 'I'm tempted to fit a couple of bolts to this door, too.'

Jemma swallowed. 'What is it? What have I brought back?'

'It is a very ancient, very evil book,' said Raphael, 'and I'm not saying any more than that.' He strode across the room and filled the kettle. 'I need a strong cup of tea, and I dare say you all do too.'

Without a word, Luke fetched his drinks bottle, took the top off, and drained it.

***

'That book should never have been in the London Library,' said Raphael, as they sat round the table in the café downstairs, nursing mugs of tea. Folio and Luna sat on the café counter, tails curled around their paws, watching proceedings. 'I would never have allowed a book like that to be stored anywhere except in a secure repository. And when I say secure, I mean a Keeper's repository.'

Jemma glanced at Maddy. 'Thank heavens I didn't show you the book when you asked.'

139

'Frankly, I have no idea how you managed to capture that book, Jemma.' Raphael looked serious. 'At least you had the tongs and the gauntlets, I suppose.'

'But I didn't,' said Jemma. 'I mean, I did, but the shelves were so crammed that I couldn't get hold of it. So I took off the gauntlet and grabbed it.'

Raphael's eyebrows shot up. 'You . . . grabbed it?' He put his mug on the table. 'Show me your hands.'

Jemma put her hands on the table, palms up. 'It was really hot. I thought I'd burnt myself, but after a while it sort of . . . went off.'

'It went off.' Raphael examined her hands carefully, turning her thumbs and fingertips this way and that. 'I see.' He swallowed. 'Well, no harm done. Good.' He picked up his mug and took several gulps.

Jemma looked at him for some time without speaking. 'Do you think it was a Grade Two emergency?' she asked. 'That's what Jasper thought.'

Raphael set his mug down and shook his head. 'No, that wasn't a Grade Two.' He sighed. 'It was a Grade One. That worries me a great deal. There hasn't been a Grade One knowledge emergency in Westminster for a good forty years. If there's another one, and this bookshop isn't here to contain it, I have no idea what will happen. But it won't be good.'

They sat in silence for a moment, digesting this. Em was first to speak. 'I'm new to this,' she said, 'but if this is a Grade One, then how did Jemma—'

'No idea,' said Raphael. 'That book, that deadly book, should not have been in the London Library. Someone

140

brought it in and planted it deliberately, to cause trouble.'

Jemma frowned. 'But how—'

'I don't know!' cried Raphael. 'Consider this, though. When the knowledge emergency happened, who did Jasper call?'

'You, of course,' said Jemma.

'Exactly. He called me. It was only chance that I was unavailable and you went instead.' He swallowed. 'I'm going to tell you something, but first you must all swear that you will never speak of it outside these four walls.'

'I swear,' said Jemma.

'We swear,' said Luke and Maddy.

'I swear,' said Carl.

Em looked at Jemma, then nodded. 'I swear.'

Raphael studied them all in turn. 'Good.' He took a deep breath. 'The book currently residing in our stockroom is extremely rare. Very few copies remain in existence. Most have been destroyed, and others have self-destructed. Sometimes they catch fire spontaneously and reduce themselves to ashes; sometimes they vanish, leaving a little pile of silvery dust. I shall not tell you the name of the book; but I will tell you that it deals with a subject concerning which I have a certain . . . weakness. To my knowledge, Armand Dupont is the only living person aware of this weakness, since I had to disclose it under the terms of my employment. I thought everyone else aware of it was dead. This incident, however, suggests I was wrong.'

Jemma laid a hand on his arm. 'What does this mean, Raphael?'

Raphael finished his drink and put the mug down. 'My

141

belief is that someone who knows of my weakness planted that book, hoping I would come to the London Library, leaving the safety and protection of my own bookshop, and handle it. Depending on the conditions, and the level of precaution I took, the best-case scenario is that I would have been . . . damaged.'

'And the worst-case scenario?' Jemma whispered.

Raphael shrugged. 'I would have died.' He pinched the bridge of his nose. 'It all makes sense now: the transport hub, the compulsory purchase order, the war on the bookshop. Someone wants to destroy the bookshop, and someone wants to destroy me.'

Chapter 18

Luke was the first to break the silence. 'Do you think...
Has Brian come back?'

'I doubt that's possible,' said Raphael. 'Armand Dupont
himself banished Brian from the Keeper's Guild, and from
contacting or speaking to anyone within it.'

'He did,' said Jemma. 'I was there. And this doesn't
feel like Brian.' She turned to Luke. 'What do you think?
You know him better than any of us, seeing as he's your
great-great-nephew and all.'

'True,' said Luke. 'You're right. I just tend to assume
that whenever something bad happens, Brian is at the
bottom of it.' He pushed his flop of dark hair off his
forehead. 'But if it isn't Brian, then who's doing this?'

'Good question,' said Raphael. 'I'd love to be able to
say that I don't have any enemies, but unfortunately I have
plenty. When you've been around as long as I have, and got

on the wrong side of several people who also aren't dying any time soon, people who wish you ill do tend to accumulate.'

Em beckoned Jemma closer and whispered in her ear. 'How old is Raphael?'

Jemma whispered back, 'We're not exactly sure, but at least three hundred and fifty.' She looked at Em to judge the effect of this information, but disappointingly, Em seemed to take it in her stride.

She turned her attention to the matter in hand. 'We must work out where the trouble is coming from. We know Mr Bunce and Mr Tipping want to get their hands on the bookshop, for instance.'

'I reckon we can count Mr Tipping out,' said Carl. 'He's Bunce's yes-man.'

'I agree,' said Raphael. 'And Bunce is certainly a malevolent sort of chap, but I can't see him smuggling a book into the London Library. It's much more his style to strangle me with red tape.'

'Yeah,' said Em. 'He comes across as someone who's focused on getting the job done and doesn't care what happens in the process, so long as he can file his paperwork.'

'So he might be implicated, we're saying,' said Jemma, 'but he's not the main villain. Then who is?'

Maddy shrugged. 'Maybe someone at the council who's deliberately keeping out of sight.'

'Could be,' said Jemma. 'Em, you've seen the plans and the consultation documents. Can you remember anything?'

Em's mouth twisted. 'The thing about that sort of stuff

is that they don't normally put names on it. The chief executive or the chairperson or whoever signs it off, and then it's anonymous.' She thought for a moment. 'The Department of Transport must be involved, because it's a transport hub, and then there's DZD Holdings, who are building it.'

'DZD Holdings…' said Raphael. 'I hadn't heard of them before this. Had anyone else?'

They all looked at each other, then shook their heads.

'That's interesting in itself,' Raphael continued. 'If they're taking on a project of this size, they must be big enough to have a record at Companies House.'

'Good point,' said Em. 'I can check if you like. And I bet they've got a website.' She glanced at Jemma. 'What do you think, Jemma?'

Jemma jumped. 'Sorry, Em, I just thought of something. Raphael, how long do you think that book was in the London Library before it started, um, making its presence felt?'

'Not long,' said Raphael. 'I imagine it was brought in a protective case and conveyed into the reading room in a pocket, since bags aren't allowed. Once that book was removed from its case and juxtaposed with other books, it would take perhaps a few minutes for it to orient itself in its surroundings, then begin to react. That time would lengthen if the room was comparatively quiet and no one was in the vicinity.'

Jemma thought. 'So if no one was on the walkway…'

'That would slow things down,' said Raphael. 'In addition, the initial signs of reaction would be slight: the book warming up, a subtle change in the quality of the air surrounding it, an occasional small localised tremor.' He paused, thinking. 'If everyone's focus was elsewhere, it might take twenty to twenty-five minutes before the book's reaction became so violent that people couldn't help noticing.'

'Right,' said Jemma. 'So the book was definitely placed in the London Library that morning? It couldn't have been there overnight, for example?'

'Absolutely not,' said Raphael. 'If it had, there wouldn't have been a library in the morning.'

'Since we know everyone who enters the library has to have a membership card,' said Jemma, 'an enquiry should give us a list of everyone who could possibly have brought in that book.' She leaned back in her chair, then sat up again. 'Do we include staff in that list?'

'It's possible a staff member could have handled the book,' said Raphael. 'On the other hand, they would still be in the library when it kicked off. Whoever did this would want to be well clear of the scene, particularly as they were, effectively, planning a murder.' He grimaced. 'How pleasant it is to contemplate one's own death.'

'Shall I make more tea?' asked Carl, gesturing to the big metal teapot which, miraculously, sat undamaged on the back counter of the café.

'I'm tempted to say yes,' said Raphael, 'but we have too much to do. There's DZD Holdings to investigate, not to mention the entry and exit records for the London Library. And I hate to broach the topic, but we've got a heck of a mess to clear up.' He looked at them all. 'Em, would you check out DZD Holdings. Jemma, Jasper Bantam owes you a considerable favour, so I'll ask you to give him a call and get those records. I suggest you both do that upstairs. Luke and Maddy, can you go to The Friendly Bookshop and check everything is in order there. If it is, open up; there's no sense in losing a whole afternoon's trading in December. Now that the bookshop isn't in imminent danger, Carl, you may head off.'

'No fear,' said Carl. 'I'm staying.'

'In that case,' said Raphael, 'I'll take up your offer of a cup of tea, since I seem to have given myself the task of tidying the mess.' He clapped his hands. 'Let's get on.' And while he spoke in his usual calm manner, everyone jumped to their feet as if he had shouted an order.

***

Em looked up from the shop laptop. 'Are you still on hold?'

'Yep,' said Jemma. 'I'm working my way through the Four Seasons. I hope I'm not at spring again before Jasper comes back on the line.' She drummed her fingers on the leather arm of the button-back chair. Luna, sitting on her lap, yawned. 'I mean, how long can it take?'

She jumped as the music cut off. 'Sorry about that,' said Jasper. 'I had a bit of trouble getting hold of the ledger. Apparently if it leaves the Issue Hall then the building might collapse.' A pause. 'That was a joke. I think.'

'OK,' said Jemma. 'I'm interested in the day when I came to the library, and in any people who had come and gone before you rang me.'

She heard rustling as Jasper turned the pages. 'Yes. Well…' He sighed. 'That's a lot of people to go through.'

'It's important, Jasper,' said Jemma. 'We need to know how that book got into the library. If we can't get hold of a list of people who could have planted it there, we'll have to launch a full-scale investigation.' She had a sudden thought. 'Nobody could have sneaked in, could they?'

'Absolutely not,' said Jasper indignantly. 'We are very mindful of security.' He heaved a sigh hard enough to blow his ledger away. 'All right, I'll start reading. Do you have a pen and paper handy?'

Jemma reached under Luna and pulled out her notepad, which was now rather warm, and retrieved a Pencil of Truth from the crevice between the cushions. 'OK, I'm ready.' She listened and took down names. 'Yep . . . yes . . . got that…' Her pencil, poised to write the next name, froze. 'Could you repeat that, please? Yes, got it.' She wrote two more names. 'You're sure that's everyone?'

'Oh yes,' said Jasper. 'People tend to stay for a good long time, you see, once they get in. We're not the sort of library you pop into for one book.'

'Except when you do,' said Jemma. 'Thanks, Jasper, that's really helpful.'

'No problem,' said Jasper. 'And if you need to ask any questions, *you* could always pop in. We could have coffee —'

'That would be lovely,' said Jemma. 'I must go, but thank you again.' She ended the call and stared into space.

'I can't decide whether you've had a breakthrough or lost the plot,' said Em.

'I should have known,' said Jemma. 'Not that I can prove anything yet, but when I do... Anyway, how's your search going?'

Em ran her hand along the top of the screen. 'They're a construction company,' she said. 'Quite well-established; they've been going for twenty-five years. They're independent, they're solvent, and they specialise in underground stuff. Shoring up buildings, subways, large basement extensions, that sort of thing.'

'Makes sense that they'd be involved with a subterranean transport hub, then,' Jemma remarked.

'Yes, completely,' Em replied. 'The board of directors is exactly the lineup of men in suits you'd expect. They've all been in construction for their whole career, except a couple who have come from manufacturing or other branches of engineering.' She shrugged. 'There really isn't much to say.' She clicked on the mouse pad. 'Oh!'

'What is it?' Jemma sat up, nearly upsetting Luna, who gave her a reproachful look.

'I clicked on the link for board papers, and apparently there is an extraordinary board meeting today.' Em clicked again. 'This agenda says the first part of the meeting is open to the public, and the transport hub is item two.' Her eyes met Jemma's over the laptop screen. 'We should go. We can ask questions, or raise objections, or something... Oh.' Her face fell.

'What's up?' Jemma persuaded Luna onto the arm of the chair and joined Em at the laptop.

'This says it starts at three o'clock, and the meeting is at their headquarters in Berkshire. It's gone two, there's no way we'll make it.'

'Don't be too sure,' said Jemma. 'Come on.'

She ran downstairs, Em in her wake, and found Raphael sitting in an armchair reading *The Colour Of Magic*, with Folio on his lap and a cup of tea at his elbow. Around him, the bookshop was immaculate.

'Sorry to disturb you,' she said, 'but we need to get Gertrude and get moving. We have a board meeting to go to, and there's no time to lose.'

Chapter 19

'There's no need to worry, Em,' said Jemma, as Gertrude took a corner on two wheels, or possibly one.

'Are you kidding?' gasped Em. One hand gripped the handle above the window, the other, her seat.

'You may not think it, but Raphael is actually a very safe driver,' said Jemma. 'And Gertrude is a very safe van. She's never crashed.'

'That makes me feel so much better,' said Em. She glanced at Carl, who was struggling to maintain his composure.

'We are going quite fast,' he muttered.

'We have to,' said Raphael, 'if we're going to make this meeting.'

'Absolutely,' said Luke. He and Maddy were sitting on one of the bench seats in the back of Gertrude, Luke's arm slung round Maddy's shoulders. Both seemed to be enjoying the ride.

'Right, everybody, hold tight,' said Raphael. 'We're heading for the motorway.'

'OoooooOH,' groaned Em.

Jemma turned round from the front passenger seat. 'If anyone wants a paper bag, I've got some in the glove box.'

'I need a distraction,' said Em. 'What's this Keeper stuff that you and Raphael talk about? What does it mean?'

'A good question, Em,' said Raphael, his eyes on the road ahead, 'but we haven't time to explain. We should arrive in ten to fifteen minutes, depending on roadworks.'

Em's eyes almost fell out of her head. 'Ten to fifteen minutes? But that's impossible!'

'Not impossible,' said Raphael. 'Just highly improbable, in a van of this age and size.' His last words were nearly drowned by the roar of Gertrude's engine as he put his foot down.

'Don't look out of the window,' said Jemma. 'You might not like it.'

Em swallowed and looked at the floor.

'Here we go,' said Raphael, a few minutes later. 'I'm taking the next exit and it's another two miles or so after that.' Gradually, Gertrude slowed to below warp speed.

The van wound along a twisting country road. 'This is a funny place for a company headquarters,' said Jemma. 'It's in the middle of nowhere.'

'Mmm,' said Em. 'That sounds suspicious to me.' She sat up from her previous slumped position and began to take an interest in her surroundings.

A few minutes later, Raphael slowed down and

indicated left. 'This would appear to be it.' Everyone craned to see as they drove into what looked like a country estate. On either side of the narrow road were undulating fields dotted with spreading trees.

'Don't get me wrong,' said Carl, 'but I was expecting a skyscraper, or an underground lair.'

'So was I,' said Jemma. The road curved round, and a sprawling half-timbered house came into view. 'I guess we were wrong.'

Raphael followed the signs for the visitors' car park, and soon Gertrude was parked alongside an array of Bentleys, Range Rovers, and Porsches. 'Arrived, and with time to spare,' he said. 'Now, equipment check. Knowledge-emergency kitbag?'

'Check,' said Jemma.

'Pencil of Truth?' He reached into his jacket pocket and produced his own.

'Oh yes,' said Jemma.

'Cinnamon rolls?'

Carl held up a bulging paper bag. 'Yes,' he said, thickly, 'minus two. Turns out they're good for travel sickness.'

'In that case,' said Raphael, 'let's go in.'

***

'We shall proceed to item 1.3,' intoned the chairperson. 'Revision of the company's management structure.'

Jemma nudged Raphael, who jumped and sat up straight. 'Was I asleep?' he whispered.

'You were snoring,' said Jemma. 'But only quietly.'

'You know that time we saved on the journey?' muttered Carl, on her other side. 'I reckon it's been put

153

into this meeting.'

'Ssh,' Jemma replied, 'I'm trying to concentrate.' *I ought to be interested in this. Organisational structure, and all that.* But the chairperson droned on in his soothing voice about the history of the organisation, and the reason why making a minor change was extremely important, and she felt her own eyelids drooping.

She made herself sit up and studied the large mahogany table where the board sat. As Em had said, it was full of middle-aged men in suits, some with hair, some not, sitting in a wood-panelled boardroom with a high, vaulted ceiling. To reach the boardroom, they had climbed a grand staircase straight out of a stately home. *Whatever they do*, thought Jemma, *they must be good at it*. Then again, if most of your work was underground, boring was presumably an advantage. She suppressed a snigger and peeped at the other members of the public sitting on the rows of chairs around her, like an audience. They were generally well-heeled, middle-aged to slightly elderly, and had cast curious and disapproving glances at the bookshop contingent when they entered. Local people, maybe, or investors?

'And now an update on the Charing Cross transportation hub,' said the chairperson, and she jerked to attention. 'After a few setbacks due to site issues, everything appears to be proceeding smoothly, and it is envisaged we shall be able to meet the project milestones circulated in the position paper we presented at the previous meeting.' He cleared his throat. 'That is the end of the open section of this meeting,' he said, addressing the rows of seats. 'If you would leave by that door, we have refreshments waiting for you.'

'That's not fair,' muttered Em. 'What about questions?'

'I don't think they do questions,' Jemma murmured back. 'Maybe if we hang around, we can listen in.'

One of the younger men sitting at the table stood up. 'If you would come this way,' he said, with a pleasant smile, and opened the door for them to leave. Jemma was one of the last to go, and outside the door she stopped to retie the shoelace she had pulled undone a minute before. The man waited for her to finish. 'Refreshments are in the second room on the right; I'll take you down in a moment.'

'Is there a bathroom I could use?' asked Jemma, hopefully.

'Oh yes,' he said. 'We have two bathrooms opening off the refreshment room.' And he shepherded them along the corridor. Jemma noted that no sound came from the boardroom. Either the inhabitants were waiting until they had gone, or it was soundproof.

When they reached the refreshment room she pulled the others into a corner, despite Raphael's longing glances at the finger sandwiches and vol au vents. 'What are we going to do? We have to get into that meeting.'

'No chance,' said Carl. 'Check out sheepdog over there.' The man who had escorted them was consulting his watch and eyeing the door. 'I bet this place is crawling with security. I counted at least twenty cameras on the way up here.'

'Hang on a minute,' said Luke. He went to the buffet table, got a plate, and piled a handful of sandwiches on it.

He folded one into his mouth as he came back. 'Rare roast beef and horseradish,' he said. 'Lovely.'

'I'm sure it is,' said Jemma, frowning at him, 'but we're not here to enjoy the hospitality.'

'Maybe we are,' said Luke. He bolted another sandwich. 'Thing is, they'll notice if somebody tries to sneak in. But there are other ways.'

'What other ways?' asked Jemma, as Luke stuffed another sandwich into his mouth.

'I think I understand,' said Raphael. He cupped his hand to Luke's ear and whispered.

Luke nodded. 'That's it. I haven't done it for ages, but I'll give it a try.' He drew Maddy closer and whispered to her.

She looked at him, eyes wide. 'You'd do that? For the bookshop?' She flung her arms around him.

Raphael leaned down to Jemma and whispered, 'Luke will assume bat form.'

'Oh,' said Jemma, staring at Luke. 'Wow.'

'So this is the plan,' said Luke, once he'd finished his fifth sandwich. 'Maddy and I leave: I need someone to mind my clothes, and obviously I can't do this here. I'll do my best to get in – if I can't, I'll come back. You stay until they kick you out, then return to Gertrude, and Maddy and I will join you there. I hope.'

'Excellent,' said Raphael, and wandered over to the buffet table.

Jemma gazed at Luke as he wolfed yet another sandwich. 'I feel as if I should shake your hand, or hug you, or something.'

156

'Don't worry,' said Maddy, laying her hand on Luke's arm. 'I'll do all that.' She gazed at Luke, starry-eyed. 'Are you sure you don't mind me seeing?'

Luke played with the end of her plait. 'As long as you're OK with it.'

'Of course I am,' she said. 'It's part of who you are.' Her eyes sparkled. 'Come on, let's go.'

***

Jemma glanced at the luminous hands of the clock on Gertrude's dashboard. 'That's an hour now.' She bit her lip. 'I hope they're OK.' It was almost dark outside, and their van was alone in the visitors' car park.

'I'm sure they will be,' said Raphael. 'Another cinnamon roll, Em?'

'No, thank you,' said Em. She looked both perturbed and utterly weary, since Raphael, Jemma and Carl had spent most of the past hour explaining the properties of the bookshop and the Keeper's Guild. 'You know, if I hadn't seen what happened in the bookshop earlier, I'd think you were all living in a fantasy world.'

'Perhaps we are,' said Raphael. 'But you have to admit it's a pretty good one.'

They jumped at a bang on Gertrude's side. Carl opened the door and Maddy scrambled in. 'Start the engine,' she said, 'but keep the lights off. Luke is just getting dressed, and then he'll be here.'

They waited, listening. Three minutes later they heard the faintest tap. Maddy opened the door and pulled him inside.

'How did it go?' asked Jemma. His expression was hard

157

to make out in the dark van.

'They want the bookshop,' said Luke. 'They don't care about the rest of the shops in the parade, and the transport hub's a front. They'll build it if they have to, but their plan is to get the bookshop, then stage an accident that will destroy everything. She said she didn't want a brick left whole.'

'She?' said Jemma. 'Who do you mean? There weren't any women in the boardroom, apart from in the audience.'

'I didn't catch her name,' said Luke. 'It took me a little while to transform and then find a way into the rafters. It's easier to turn into several bats, you see, because of the body-mass issue, and only half of us went in: a large group of bats might have been conspicuous. We couldn't hear everything, but what we did hear was pretty damning. When the meeting finished, she took a couple of people aside and said, "Let's discuss this at my place."'

'Could you see much?' asked Jemma.

'A reasonable amount,' said Luke. 'Bats can see quite well, you know. It was a bit bright in there, though, so we couldn't look for too long. She was blonde, wearing an expensive suit. She was clearly in charge.'

'I bet she was,' said Jemma. 'Tell me, did she sound posh?'

'Yeah,' said Luke. 'Really posh.'

'In that case,' said Jemma, 'I know who she is.' Her fists clenched. 'She gave apologies for the management strategies meeting last Thursday. I thought it was because she couldn't be bothered to attend, but she *was* busy. She was busy planting that book in the London Library. She's one of Brian's associates, and it sounds as if she's striking out on her own.'

'Well, come on then,' said Em. 'Who is it?'

'Drusilla Davenport,' said Jemma. 'DZD Holdings. Her bookshop's in the next town. We must follow her.'

Raphael switched on Gertrude's headlights and put the van into gear.

'There's a problem,' whispered Maddy.

Even in the dimly lit van, Jemma could see how pale she was. 'What is it?'

'Look.' Maddy laid her hand on Luke's, and it sank in further than a hand should. Jemma peered at Luke: his form was – not transparent, but slightly less solid than usual. 'What's happened?' Maddy asked, in a shocked whisper.

'It's OK,' said Luke, though he appeared anything but. 'One of my bats has a terrible sense of direction, and he's wandered off somewhere. It's happened before.' He swallowed, looking nauseous. 'But that doesn't matter. We need to find Drusilla, and put a stop to this for good.'

Chapter 20

'How do we find out where Drusilla lives?' said Jemma. She looked at Raphael. 'Unless you happen to know.'

'It's probably in the files somewhere,' said Raphael. 'Though, of course, they may not be up to date. One of those jobs I always mean to get round to and never do.' He leaned forward and pushed the button under the steering wheel. They heard a click, and the clock on Gertrude's dashboard swung on a hinge to reveal a round grey screen, like a tiny round television. Raphael leaned forward and said, very loudly and distinctly, 'Drusilla.' Then he sat back and folded his arms.

An arrow pointing left appeared, and Gertrude's steering wheel spun.

'You never told me Gertrude had a satnav,' said Jemma. 'Or that she can drive herself.'

'I try not to use it too often,' said Raphael. 'I wouldn't

want to get lazy.'

Jemma rolled her eyes.

Gertrude nosed her way out of the visitors' car park, down the drive, and onto the main road.

'Maybe Drusilla will have a skyscraper or an underground lair,' Carl said hopefully.

'I hope not,' said Jemma. 'Anyway, what do we do when we get there?'

They all looked at Raphael, who seemed intent on the road ahead. Eventually, he sensed the silence and glanced round at them.

'What do we do?' repeated Jemma. A thought struck her. 'You don't think she'll challenge you, do you?' She remembered the day when Brian had arrived at the bookshop to do just that – the verbal fencing, the grandstanding, the slow, deliberate unveiling of the books. Since Drusilla had set up a whole company and secured the contract for a transport hub just to weaken Raphael, Jemma dreaded to think what else she might have in mind.

'Challenge me?' said Raphael. 'She can't: the challenger visits the incumbent's location. Which is as well, because I doubt I'd win a challenge with an *AA Road Atlas* and a *London A-Z*.'

'Ah,' said Jemma, feeling not at all reassured. 'So what do we do when we get there?'

'Confront her,' said Raphael.

'We can't,' said Jemma. 'We don't have any proof. I mean, yes, Luke's heard plenty, but it's hardly admissible in a court of law—'

'We aren't a court of law,' said Raphael, 'and a good

161

thing too. What Luke has told us, along with the circumstantial evidence regarding the London Library, is more than enough to proceed. Besides, I don't think Drusilla will deny anything. In fact, I'm probably playing right into her hands.'

Jemma put a hand on his arm. 'Then why are we doing this?'

Raphael's face took on a look of stern resolution. 'I know now that Drusilla wants to destroy me. At first I thought someone wanted to weaken me through the bookshop, but no. That book—' He shuddered. 'Presumably she knows I survived, but not how. It's only a matter of time before she tries again, and perhaps next time I shall not be so lucky. I refuse to live in fear. If I can confront her before she grows stronger still, perhaps I have a chance.'

Jemma stared at him. 'But—'

'No. My mind is made up.'

'And what happens if you don't win?' Jemma cried. 'What if *she* wins?'

Raphael's mouth twitched. 'I don't know. If she does win, I doubt I'll be in a state to care.' He paused. 'Let's not be too negative. I still have a few tricks up my sleeve.'

'I hope so,' said Jemma, as Gertrude slowed down. A picture of a large stone house appeared on the screen, with an arrow pointing left, and the caption *200 metres*.

***

'I still don't see why you have to come,' said Raphael, rather sourly, as they edged across the lawn in front of the house.

162

'We're not letting you do this alone,' said Jemma.

'No, absolutely not,' said Carl. He glanced at Em. 'I bet this wasn't in the job description.'

Em shook her head and kept trudging.

'Luke,' said Raphael, as they neared the house, 'can you remember what the two men looked like? The ones that Drusilla invited?'

Luke thought. 'One was the chairperson of the meeting,' he said, 'and the other wore a pinstripe suit with a red tie.'

'I remember the chairperson,' said Raphael. 'I spent a lot of time staring at him and wondering how anyone could be so dull.'

They were almost at the house. Two cars were parked outside: a red Porsche with the number plate DZD1, and a black Bentley. 'One's here, one isn't,' said Raphael. 'Keep out of the light.' He walked behind a large tree at the edge of the lawn. A minute or so later, the grey-haired, slightly tubby, suited form of the chairperson walked out.

'How did he do that?' whispered Em.

'I didn't know he *could* do that,' Jemma replied. She shivered; she felt as though an icicle were freezing her from the inside.

She watched as the chairperson – *no, not the chairperson, it's Raphael* – walked up to the front door and rang the bell. They heard the crackle of a loudspeaker, then a click. Raphael pushed the door open and beckoned them in.

Drusilla's hall was much as Jemma would have expected: luxurious, yet cold and minimal. A high ceiling, a marble floor, modern art on the walls. 'They're in the drawing room, apparently,' said Raphael.

'Who has a drawing room?' whispered Carl, sounding both impressed and disgusted.

Voices were coming from the room on the right; Drusilla's cut-glass tones tinkled.

'All of you face that wall,' said Raphael. 'I can't stay like this much longer.' After a pause, he said, 'All done,' and when they turned back, Raphael looked just as usual. *Or does he?* thought Jemma. She peered at him, trying to work out what the difference was. If anything, it was that he seemed more tired than before.

'Come on,' said Raphael, and opened the door.

Drusilla was sitting, legs crossed, on a shiny black chesterfield sofa, and opposite her was the chairperson from the meeting. 'Oh, Raphael,' she said. 'What a pleasant surprise.' Her tone didn't match her words at all. 'Or should I say, not a surprise. I see you've brought your . . . gang with you.'

'I know what you've been doing, Drusilla,' said Raphael, his voice low and angry, 'and it must stop.'

'I take it this is the bookshop chap,' said the chairperson, looking pleased. 'I wondered what he was like.'

'Now you know,' said Drusilla. 'So weak that he has to resort to a mob to provide him with moral support.'

'Oh dear,' said the chairperson. 'Shall I wait in the other room?'

He made to get up, but Drusilla raised a hand. 'No, Philip, you may stay. Raphael has brought his witnesses, and I shall have mine.' She turned to Raphael. 'So what exactly do you plan to do?'

'If you wish to challenge me,' said Raphael, 'you may. There is no point in me using the official channels; by the time that's done I won't have a bookshop, and that's exactly what you want.'

Drusilla raised an eyebrow. 'Don't flatter yourself, Raphael. I'm not interested in you; I'm interested in your position. You're so weak, and you rule from a position of weakness. Letting some jumped-up shopgirl dictate the way you run things?' Her lip curled as she glanced at Jemma. 'I daresay your uncle is spinning in his grave.'

'Leave my uncle out of this,' Raphael said, clenching his jaw.

'Brian told me he could bring you down,' said Drusilla. 'Foolishly, I believed him. I even gave him my support. But he was as weak as you in the end. I should have listened to my instincts, and used the connections and the expertise I have built up over so many years.' She looked at Jemma again and laughed. 'Your – what is it – five years of work experience? Hah! I have coiled myself around London like a serpent, Raphael; you could not disentangle me if you tried. And I mean to have my way.'

'That won't happen, Drusilla,' said Raphael. 'You'll regret this.'

Drusilla smiled a slow smile that chilled Jemma to the marrow. 'I don't think so.' She paused, considering. 'Perhaps I shall challenge you. Not with books – no, you know all the loopholes, all the little dodges that helped you claim that spurious victory over Brian. No, we should do something different. Something more . . . suitable. This isn't just about books any more, is it? It's about power. And your power is waning.' She sneered at him. 'Look at you, so old, so tired. Your little deception at the door must have taken its toll. Especially given your . . . weakness.'

'How do you know about that?' snapped Raphael.

'I've known of your predilection for shifting for many years,' said Drusilla. 'Once upon a time, a retired Assistant Keeper in a remote part of the country owed me a favour. He was very old, and came from a bookish family. Conscious of his unpaid debt, he vouchsafed the information on his deathbed, and I have kept it safe ever since.' She smiled. 'Until now.'

Drusilla stood up and walked to the edge of a large round silvery-beige rug in the middle of the floor. She kicked off her high-heeled shoes and stepped onto the edge. 'I challenge you to a battle of wills,' she said. 'It shouldn't take long. Did you like my little surprise at the London Library?'

'You've convicted yourself out of your own mouth, Drusilla,' said Raphael. 'But very well. I accept.' He took off his jacket, handed it to Carl, and began to roll up his sleeves.

'Don't do this,' said Jemma. 'There must be another way.' Drusilla was watching Raphael as a cat watches a mouse. *Do something.*

Maddy took Raphael's arm, but he gently disengaged her.

'Seriously, Raphael, this is such a bad idea,' said Carl.

'I hope you won't let them talk you out of it,' said

166

Drusilla, eyes gleaming.

'There's no need,' said Jemma. She bent, pulled her trainers off, and stepped onto the edge of the rug opposite Drusilla. 'I stand in Raphael's place.'

Chapter 21

'Are you crazy?' Carl cried. 'What do you think you're doing?'

'I'm stepping in,' said Jemma. 'Literally.'

'Please don't, Jemma,' said Raphael. 'Please step off that rug.'

'Think about it, Raphael,' said Jemma. 'Even if I don't win, I'll weaken her – maybe enough to stop this. Even if I don't, we've lost nothing. You can still challenge her afterwards, if you have to.' She folded her arms. 'I'm not moving.'

'This is an unexpected development,' said Drusilla, grinning. 'I didn't expect you to put your underling into the ring, Raphael.'

'He didn't,' said Jemma. 'I'm doing this of my own free will.'

'She is,' said Em. 'And I believe in her. I believe Jemma

can do this.'

I'm glad you believe in me, thought Jemma, *because I'm not sure I do.*

'I believe Jemma can do it, too,' said Maddy. 'You'd better watch out, Drusilla.' She smacked her fist into her palm and Luke gave her a surprised glance.

'Um, what exactly is going to happen?' said Philip. 'Are you fighting, or what?'

Drusilla snorted. 'Honestly, Philip, there's no need to get excited. We fight each other with the mind. We marshal our mental powers against each other, with the aim of forcing our opponent out of the arena of combat. Whoever is the last in the circle – or in this case, on the rug – wins.'

'So it's like sumo wrestling, then,' said Philip, 'but non-contact.'

Drusilla sighed. 'I suppose so. If you must think of it in those terms. Right, then – what's your name again?'

Jemma uncrossed her arms and faced Drusilla. 'My name is Jemma James. You know that. Don't try to intimidate me.'

'That's actually quite scary,' Luke whispered to Maddy.

'Have you done this before?' asked Drusilla.

Jemma shook her head.

'I didn't think so. Touching your opponent in any way is absolutely forbidden. You may speak, but your main weapon is your mind. No one from outside the circle may intervene. No gestures, no speaking, and of course no touching.'

'And what does the winner get?' asked Jemma.

Drusilla's mouth curled up at the corners. 'Nothing.

The loser, however, having proved themselves an unfit opponent and therefore unworthy, leaves their position.' Her smile broadened and her eyes gleamed. 'Assuming they are still alive.'

Carl winced. 'It's not too late, Jemma. You can still step out. Please don't do this—'

'I said I'd do it, and I'm doing it.' Jemma took a step forward and Drusilla did the same.

'Jemma, you can do this,' said Em. 'You're stronger than you think; you always have been. People have tried to stand in your way, or knock you down, and you come back every time. You don't win every battle, but you win the war. You're the most resilient person I know.' She laid a hand on Jemma's shoulder. 'Use your strength.'

'Thank you,' said Jemma, and faced Drusilla. 'I'm ready.' She stared into Drusilla's hazel eyes. *Don't let Drusilla inside your head. Keep her out, and push into hers. Find her weakness.*

'We fight to the end,' said Drusilla. 'May the best woman win.' She stared back at Jemma. 'Let us begin.'

Jemma braced herself, expecting to be hit by an invisible force that would make her reel. Instead she felt as if she were breathing in a thin vapour. It reminded her of the wisp of dark, oily smoke from the book at the London Library. *Be careful.*

'You're very silly,' said Drusilla, with regret in her voice. 'Thinking that you can win. Many people have tried to overcome me, and no one has succeeded. People have fallen to their knees and begged for mercy on this rug.' She smiled in a way that made it clear she had never granted it.

'I have seen and withstood things you cannot imagine.'

'I'm sure you have, but I don't care,' said Jemma, and her voice sounded much more confident than she felt. 'You won't win. What you're planning is evil.'

'It isn't evil,' said Drusilla, 'it's necessary. It's time this tired old man gave up his throne. It's time for a new age: a powerful, decisive age.'

'An age where you'll be in charge, I suppose,' said Jemma. 'Maybe you won't find that as easy as you think. Do you realise that, apart from your cronies, people don't like you?'

'I'm not here to be liked,' said Drusilla. 'I'm here to do my job. I'm here to run things the way they should be run, not give in to people and allow standards to fall.'

'Your standards are outdated,' said Jemma. 'You're out of touch. The world has moved on without you.'

'Then perhaps it's time to move it back,' said Drusilla. 'You can bamboozle Raphael with your buzzwords and your jargon, Jemma James, but I can read you like a book. And I won't let such a silly little thing get in my way.' Her voice was low, gentle, almost soothing, but every word dripped with poison.

Jemma's head felt so full of smoke that it might burst. She rubbed her forehead to clear the pressure. *I need something to shield my mind, like the handkerchief at the library.* She visualised a clean white handkerchief wrapping itself around her brain, and the fog began to clear.

She focused on Drusilla, who stood with her head held high. 'I am getting in your way,' she said, 'because you're

171

doing wrong, and we have to stop you. Raphael's bookshop is more important than you or me. It helps keep London safe. It helps keep the country safe. With you in charge, Drusilla, there would be no safety. Instead, there would be tyranny, cruelty, and terror.'

She took another step forward. 'You baited a trap for Raphael: a trap that could have killed him. And not just him, but anyone else unfortunate enough to be in the wrong place at the wrong time. How could you do such a despicable thing?'

Drusilla laughed. 'I'm only sorry that I didn't kill him,' she said. 'If anyone else had died…' She shrugged. 'A casualty of war. Inevitable, really.' She smiled. 'No matter. I have weakened Raphael sufficiently to make you step up in his place. You'll regret that by the time I've finished with you.'

Jemma looked into Drusilla's face. 'Did you weaken Raphael, though? You see, Raphael didn't take the call from the London Library. I did.'

Drusilla's eyebrows drew together.

'I went to the library, I found the book, I took it from the shelf with my bare hands, and I removed it to a place of safety. And I have every intention of removing you, too.' She fixed her gaze on a spot between Drusilla's arched eyebrows and imagined prodding it with her forefinger. *Jab.*

Drusilla blinked.

'You didn't like that, did you?' Jemma raised her right hand and visualised laying her palm against Drusilla's forehead. In her mind, she gave a little push.

172

Drusilla's head snapped back. She glanced behind her, then at Jemma, her expression no longer confident. 'I don't believe you,' she said. 'You had help.'

'I had a handkerchief and a lead-lined box,' said Jemma. 'If you don't believe me, ask Jasper Bantam, or any of the readers who were there. They all saw me do it. Unlike you, because you ran away scared.' She held up her hands and imagined gripping Drusilla's shoulders.

Drusilla swallowed. 'If this is true,' she said, 'maybe we can work together. You could be my second in command. You'd own a bookshop; you wouldn't be an employee any more. You'd like that, wouldn't you?'

'That won't ever happen, Drusilla,' said Jemma. 'I despise you. I despise what you stand for, and I'm going to push you out. You're clever, you're cunning, but I want nothing to do with you.' Hands still raised, she took a step forward.

Drusilla's jaw dropped. 'What – I don't – stop it!' She put her own hands up and tried to resist, but her shoulders were straining backwards and she had to follow. She took a step back, then another, her feet almost hidden in the deep pile of the rug.

Jemma took step after inexorable step until Drusilla staggered away and one foot, then the other, touched the floor.

A pin dropping would have sounded like the clang of a bell. Drusilla righted herself then stood silent, arms hanging by her sides. She gave Philip a quick, nervous glance. Then she put her shoes on, but while they made her taller, somehow she seemed to have shrunk. It was as if

173

her soul had left the room, and only the husk of her remained.

'I don't think anything else will happen, Jemma,' said Raphael quietly. 'But just in case, don't turn your back on her.'

'Can I step off the rug?' asked Jemma. She realised she was sweating.

Raphael looked rather surprised. 'Yes, of course.'

'Was that it?' asked Carl.

'It was,' said Raphael. 'Well done, Jemma.' He gave her a one-armed hug. 'Obviously, Philip – may I call you Philip? – this nonsense with the transport hub must be called off. Actually, no. If the public want it, you may build it, but it will have to be somewhere else. Do I make myself clear?'

Philip straightened his tie. 'Um—'

'You see, given what we overheard at the board meeting earlier, and what Drusilla has admitted in front of witnesses, we have more than enough evidence to bring a case against you,' said Raphael. 'I'm sure you wouldn't want that to happen.'

'Absolutely not,' said Philip. 'Understood.'

'Good,' said Raphael. He turned back to Drusilla. 'Your position as Assistant Keeper and member of the Keepers' Guild is hereby rescinded, Drusilla,' he said. 'You may keep your bookshop, but it will be subject to inspection. If I find any irregularities, or mistreatment of your staff or your resources, there will be consequences.'

Drusilla said nothing.

'I'm sorry it had to end this way,' said Raphael.

Drusilla glanced at him, then Jemma, her face expressionless. Jemma tried not to shiver when Drusilla's eyes met hers; she showed no sign of emotion, understanding, or even recognition. Jemma could have been a lamp post in the street. 'We'll see ourselves out, shall we,' Jemma said, slipping her feet into her shoes and bending to lace them, glad to escape the gaze of those empty eyes.

They filed from the room, not sure what else to say or what could be said, and the front door shut behind them with a decisive click.

'Well, that was something,' said Raphael. 'Are you all right, Jemma?'

'Yes, I'm fine,' said Jemma, automatically. *I am fine,* she told herself.

'I said you could do it,' said Em, giving her a squeeze.

'You did. Thanks.' Jemma slipped an arm around Em's waist. 'I'm glad it's over.'

'It was amazing,' said Carl. 'But also very weird.' He shot her a look. 'You're not going to do that mind stuff on me, are you?'

'It wouldn't work if I tried,' said Jemma. They laughed, and carried on walking towards Gertrude. 'Let's go home.'

'Good idea,' said Luke. 'Somewhere there's a rare steak with my name on it.'

Carl made a face. 'I'd rather go for pizza.'

'Not just yet,' said Jemma, opening the passenger-side door. 'First, we've got cats to feed.'

Chapter 22

Raphael raised his glass. 'Cheers!'

'Cheers!' echoed the staff and the customers, in a ragged chorus. 'Merry Christmas!'

'And this time we won't get interrupted,' Jemma murmured to Carl.

'No chance,' he replied. 'Not now the transport hub's off. Funny, that.' He grinned. That morning the local paper had published an exclusive story that the transport hub had been found to be unviable, and therefore would not be going ahead.

'So all that work to get listed-building status for the shop was for nothing,' said Em, downcast.

'Don't say that,' said Raphael. 'It's something to be proud of, and hopefully it will protect us in the future.'

'Let's hope so,' said Jemma. 'I know you've thrown Drusilla out of her job and the Keepers' Guild, but I don't think she's finished.' She could still see Drusilla's empty hazel eyes looking back at her.

'Perhaps she has,' said Raphael. 'An advertisement for a bookshop for sale in Windsor popped up this lunchtime.'

'Mmm,' said Jemma. 'I wouldn't be too sure—' She broke off as a black blur streaked past her, followed by a ginger one. 'Those cats!'

'They're just having fun,' said Maddy. 'The customers love them.'

Luna skidded to a halt at the fantasy section, put her front paws on the shelf, and nosed at the Neil Gaimans. Folio stood nearby, watching her.

'I think they like each other,' said Maddy.

'Yes, it's nice that they're friends,' said Jemma.

Maddy shot her a look. 'I mean *like* each other.'

'Oh, don't. Luna's too young.'

'Mmm,' said Maddy, and slipped an arm through Luke's.

Jemma turned to Carl. He was studying Em, who had gone behind the counter to make coffee for a customer. 'She's very much at home, isn't she?' he said. 'In my old place.'

'She is,' said Jemma. 'Do you miss it?'

Carl sighed. 'More than I thought I would.' He put an arm round Jemma. 'I've loved doing the play, and it's great that we have another run booked in January . . . but it's not the same.'

'No,' said Jemma. 'But does it have to be?' She glanced in Em's direction. 'Back in a moment.'

She went to the counter and waited her turn. 'What'll it

be?' said Em.

'Nothing to drink,' said Jemma. 'I'm sorry.'

Em stared at her. 'What for?'

'For being horrible when you came back, and not telling the truth about the shop. I was still angry with you and I let it get to me.' She held out her hand. 'Are we friends?'

Em shook the outstretched hand. 'Yes, we are. I understand why you were angry.' She looked down. 'I wasn't completely truthful about why I came back, either. I did want to prove Damon wrong, but . . . I wanted to make peace with you too.' She smiled. 'And I missed London. I didn't plan to come and work in your bookshop, but I saw the advert and – it was just how things turned out.'

'Maybe they turned out for the best,' said Jemma.

'Maybe,' said Em. 'Although you're not the person you were when I left. Quite apart from the magical powers.'

Jemma frowned. 'What do you mean?'

Em shrugged. 'It's hard to say, exactly. More self-assured, maybe.'

'Me?' said Jemma. 'I'm the least self-assured person anywhere—'

Upstairs, a doorbell rang.

'That's odd,' said Em. 'I didn't know we had a doorbell.'

'We do,' said Jemma, 'but it's so well hidden that most people knock.' She frowned. 'Let's hope Bunce and Tipping haven't decided to gatecrash.'

'I'd better go and see,' said Luke, from a quiet corner. He put his glass on the counter and headed for the door.

'Not on your own, you're not,' said Jemma. 'I'm coming too.' That day they had had to keep the lights low in the shop to prevent customers noticing Luke's slight transparency, and he was on light duties, much to his disgust.

She ran upstairs just in time to see Luke open the door and look into the street. 'There's no one there – oh!' Jemma followed his gaze. Lying at his feet was a small, crumpled bat. 'He made it!' Gently he picked up the little creature in both hands and brought him into the shop.

'Is he hurt?' asked Jemma, closing the door and following Luke. 'He's flown a long way. Should we give him milk, or bread and water, or . . . something?'

The bat managed a feeble flutter. 'Don't worry,' said Luke. He opened the door to the staff bathroom. 'Back in a moment.'

Jemma waited outside, wondering what was going on. A minute or so later, the door opened. 'That's much better,' said Luke. He breathed out, and a slow smile spread over his face. 'See?' He held his hand out to Jemma and she realised she couldn't see through it. She gave his hand an experimental poke, and it felt just as a hand should.

'That's brilliant!' She flung her arms around him. 'I'm so glad!'

'So am I,' said Luke, with feeling. 'It's no fun being not quite all there. Last night I dreamt about woods, and drizzle, and soaring over motorways…' He grinned. 'I'll go and tell Maddy.' He headed for the stairs.

Jemma heard an 'Oops, sorry,' and Raphael appeared.

'Everything all right?' he asked.

'More than all right. Luke's missing bat came home!'

'I know,' said Raphael. 'He bumped into me.' He studied Jemma. 'Anyway, I meant you. You've been a bit quiet ever since we returned from Drusilla's.'

'Have I?' *And I thought I'd done so well at acting normal.*

'Not quiet so much as preoccupied,' said Raphael. 'I thought it might be because you were busy, what with it being Christmas Eve, but now I think it's something else. Something a little more complicated than shopkeeping, and not quite as pleasant.'

'I'm clearly more transparent than Luke, then,' said Jemma.

'I'm afraid so,' said Raphael. 'It's to do with Drusilla, isn't it?'

Jemma nodded. 'When I was battling with her, pushing her out of that circle . . . I enjoyed it. I enjoyed having power over her. Once I got the hang of it, I knew I would win. And that scares me.'

'Yes,' said Raphael. 'It is rather frightening when you realise what you can do. That's why I didn't make too much of a fuss about you rescuing that book.' He glanced at the stockroom door. 'I still check on it every day. I should probably stop, in case it tempts me.'

It was on the tip of Jemma's tongue to ask Raphael how he had changed himself into the chairperson the day before, and how that could be a weakness, but she suppressed the urge. That conversation, if it ever happened, would be for another day. 'What do I do?' she asked. 'How do I manage it?'

'Mostly, you keep it in check,' said Raphael. 'You control it, so that it doesn't control you. Otherwise you become like Brian and Drusilla, prepared to do anything to satisfy your craving for power and your desire to exercise it constantly.'

Jemma was silent, thinking. 'Hopefully there'll be no need to exercise power now,' she said, eventually. 'The shop is safe, and you're safe, and that's what matters.'

'And you're safe too, Jemma,' said Raphael. He gave her a pat on the shoulder. 'Never forget that you have a right to be safe, and to have a life beyond the bookshop.' He paused. 'Em and Carl have noticed a difference in you.'

Jemma sighed. 'Em said. I wish people would stop worrying about me.'

'They're worrying because they care,' said Raphael. 'Let them do it, and don't push them away.' He grinned. 'Sermon over. Let's go and enjoy the rest of the party.' He led the way downstairs.

Jemma took a glass of fizz from a nearby tray and surveyed the scene. Luke and Maddy were holding each other tightly, kissing under the mistletoe. Raphael went straight to Giulia and spoke to her. She smiled at Jemma, then turned to Raphael and fed him a chocolate. Em, at the café counter, rolled her eyes at them in mock exasperation then poured herself a drink. *I'm so glad Em's here…*

'There you are,' said Carl. 'All OK?'

'Very much so,' said Jemma. 'It's lovely to have you back, at least for now.'

'It's lovely to have *you* back.' Carl kissed her, then put

181

his lips to her ear. 'Though I'm still a bit in awe of you,' he murmured. 'Not to say scared.'

'Don't be silly,' said Jemma. 'That sort of thing's just for special occasions—'

She jumped at a tiny, high-pitched meow beside her ear. She turned, expecting to see Folio, and instead came nose to nose with Luna, who was sitting on top of the bookcase.

'Was that you?' she asked, stroking the soft black fur.

Luna looked at her with big green eyes. 'Meow.'

Jemma beamed at Carl. 'She's found her meow! Go on, Luna, do another one.'

'Meow-ow,' said Luna, and swished her tail.

Carl's arms slipped around Jemma's waist. 'Perhaps she isn't the only one,' he said, and kissed her again. 'Merry Christmas, Jemma.'

Acknowledgements

As usual, my first thanks go to my super beta readers – Carol Bissett, Ruth Cunliffe, Paula Harmon, and Stephen Lenhardt – and my excellent proofreader, John Croall. As usual, any remaining errors are mine only. Thank you so much, everyone, for your support.

Additional thanks to my husband Stephen, who as ever has been supportive and encouraging, and has had to put up with me moaning about the weather much more than is usual at this time of year.

A quick note: while there is a London Library, and it may look rather like the one I've written about (virtual tours are a wonderful thing), it is not the same place and I'm sure the staff are far less officious! Maybe I'll be able to visit one day…

And my final thanks are for you, the reader. Thank you for reading, and I hope you enjoyed book 4 in the series! If you did, a short review or a rating on Amazon or Goodreads would be very much appreciated. Ratings and reviews, however short, help readers to discover books.

FONT AND IMAGE CREDITS

Cover and heading fonts: Alyssum Blossom and Alyssum Blossom Sans by Bombastype

Houses: Set of hand drawn houses by freepik: https://www.freepik.com/free-vector/set-four-hand-drawn-houses_1926210.htm

Vehicle (recoloured): Construction equipment collection Free Vector by Vintage adventure logo collection by freepik: https://www.freepik.com/free-vector/construction-equipment-collection_4621012.htm

Bat (slightly edited): taken from Happy halloween seamless illustration with the moon Free Vector by callmetak: https://www.freepik.com/free-vector/happy-halloween-seamless-illustration-with-moon_11169212.htm

Stars: Night free icon by flaticon at freepik.com: https://www.freepik.com/free-icon/night_914336.htm

Chapter vignette: Opened books in hand drawn style Free Vector by freepik at freepik.com: https://www.freepik.com/free-vector/opened-books-hand-drawn-style_765567.htm

Cover created using GIMP image editor: https://www.gimp.org

About the Author

Liz Hedgecock grew up in London, England, did an English degree, and then took forever to start writing. After several years working in the National Health Service, some short stories crept into the world. A few even won prizes. Then the stories started to grow longer…

Now Liz travels between the nineteenth and twenty-first centuries, murdering people. To be fair, she does usually clean up after herself.

Liz's reimaginings of Sherlock Holmes, the Pippa Parker cozy mystery series, the Caster & Fleet Victorian mystery series (written with Paula Harmon), the Magical Bookshop series and the Maisie Frobisher Mysteries are available in ebook and paperback.

Liz lives in Cheshire with her husband and two sons, and when she's not writing or child-wrangling you can usually find her reading, messing about on Twitter, or cooing over stuff in museums and art galleries. That's her story, anyway, and she's sticking to it.

Website/blog: http://lizhedgecock.wordpress.com
Facebook: http://www.facebook.com/lizhedgecockwrites
Twitter: http://twitter.com/lizhedgecock
Goodreads: https://www.goodreads.com/lizhedgecock
Amazon author page: http://author.to/LizH

Books by Liz Hedgecock

Short stories
The Secret Notebook of Sherlock Holmes
Bitesize
The Adventure of the Scarlet Rosebud
The Case of the Peculiar Pantomime (a Caster & Fleet short mystery)

Halloween Sherlock series (novelettes)
The Case of the Snow-White Lady
Sherlock Holmes and the Deathly Fog
The Case of the Curious Cabinet

Sherlock & Jack series (novellas)
A Jar Of Thursday
Something Blue
A Phoenix Rises

Mrs Hudson & Sherlock Holmes series (novels)
A House Of Mirrors
In Sherlock's Shadow

Pippa Parker Mysteries (novels)
Murder At The Playgroup
Murder In The Choir
A Fete Worse Than Death

Murder in the Meadow
The QWERTY Murders
Past Tense

Caster & Fleet Mysteries (with Paula Harmon)
The Case of the Black Tulips
The Case of the Runaway Client
The Case of the Deceased Clerk
The Case of the Masquerade Mob
The Case of the Fateful Legacy
The Case of the Crystal Kisses

Maisie Frobisher Mysteries (novels)
All At Sea
Off The Map
Gone To Ground
In Plain Sight

The Magical Bookshop (novels)
Every Trick in the Book
Brought to Book
Double Booked
By the Book

For children (with Zoe Harmon)
A Christmas Carrot

WHITE
RHINO
BOOKS